P9-CBB-591

Second Vespers

SECOND VESPERS

by

Ralph McInerny

A

FATHER DOWLING

Mystery

THE VANGUARD PRESS
NEW YORK

04451

Library of Congress Catalogue Card Number: 79-56379

ISBN: 0-8149-0837-3

Designer: Tom Torre Bevans

Manufactured in the United States of America.

1 2 3 4 5 6 7 8 9 0

To Pat and Jude Dougherty

Second Vespers

1

"I DON'T think he's a salesman," Marie Murkin said.

The housekeeper's voice was a husky whisper, although she had closed the door of Father Dowling's study in order to tell him he had a visitor.

"Did you ask?"

"I can tell."

Father Dowling smiled. Mrs. Murkin's certitudes were mainly negative ones and she was seldom wrong. Of course it was not much help to know only that the man awaiting him in the rectory parlor was not a salesman.

"Is there anything else he isn't, Marie?"

"Catholic."

"Oh?" Father Dowling, who had risen from his chair, book and pipe set aside, looked quizzically at Mrs. Murkin. "And how do you know that?"

"He asked for the reverend."

"Well, that's me."

"You know what I mean."

He knew what she meant. He should not tease her. She was a loyal, efficient housekeeper and a far better cook than he deserved. If she was wanting in anything, it was in a doorstep manner. Visitors to the rectory found Mrs. Murkin standing athwart their path and the burden of proof was on anyone wishing to disturb the even tenor of Father Dowling's life. It did little good to remind Mrs. Murkin that it was his job, not to say his vocation, to be available to people.

"If they ask to go to confession or anything like that, well, that's different. But most of them just want a shoulder to cry on."

"We all do."

"Hmph," said Mrs. Murkin, but he could see that she was reminded of times when even she had needed the comfort of a receptive human ear.

The young man in the front parlor was standing at a window and looking out at the grassy expanse between the rectory and church, a lawn that now in late May was greening and growing and bringing in with a vengeance that too-long-delayed spring.

"You wanted to see me?"

The young man's eyes, when he turned to Father Dowling, were moist. "My parents were married in that church."

"I see. Won't you sit down? I'm Roger Dowling."

"My name is Paul Gardiner."

After a moment's hesitation, Paul Gardiner thrust out his hand to the priest. Once seated in a chair across the desk from Roger Dowling, he put a cigarette in his mouth and struck a match. But he waved out the flame before touching it to the tip of his cigarette.

"I'm sorry, Father. I keep forgetting."

"Go ahead and smoke."

"You don't mind?"

"I smoke myself."

"A pipe?"

"Yes."

"I thought I smelled pipe smoke when I came in."

Father Dowling got comfortable in his chair, suddenly curious about this young man. If thirty can be considered young, and it certainly could be by the pastor of St. Hilary's parish in Fox River, Illinois. Roger Dowling had aged some two decades past thirty. Gardiner, with his elbows on the arms of his chair, leaned forward, his expression a peering, seemingly nearsighted one. His eyes were no longer moist. He did not seem to be enjoying the cigarette he had lit. Indeed, he seemed unsure what exactly to do with it. As for the smell of pipe smoke, well, one would have to have a legendary cold or nasal occlusion not to be overwhelmed by the lingering smell of tobacco smoke in the rectory. There had been a time when Marie Murkin had tried to keep the house fresh and antiseptically clean, but Roger Dowling's incessant puffing replaced whatever clouds of smoke she managed to drive from the house. Finally Marie decided that she liked the aroma and that it was appropriate for a priest's house to smell of tobacco. Certainly any negative comment on the tobacco odor in the rectory brought a chilly putdown from her now. For Paul Gardiner to refer to Roger Dowling's pipe smoking as to a chancy inference was surprise enough to make the young man interesting.

He said, "Everyone's gotten so moralistic about smoking lately. I've been to parties where you had to go out on the doorstep for a smoke. I think that's rude."

"Well, I suppose it's rude of us to blow smoke in people's faces."

"You sure you don't mind my smoking?"

Despite the priest's assurance, Paul Gardiner snubbed out his cigarette in the tray on the desk. Roger Dowling had the impression his caller was happy to be rid of that prop.

"Did you take a look at the church?"

Gardiner seemed startled.

"You said your parents had been married there."

"I suppose you keep records of that sort of thing?"

"Of course." Roger Dowling smiled. "Do you want a copy of your parents' marriage certificate?"

That was exactly what Paul Gardiner did want. Roger Dowling took him back to his study where the parish records were kept. The year in question was 1947.

"What was your mother's maiden name?"

"Early." Gardiner smiled a half smile. "The late Miss Early. My dad called her that. They're both that now. Late."

"I'm sorry. Do you know the date of the wedding?"

He did not. He stood beside the desk as Father Dowling turned the pages of the large ledger in which the pastor of the time had recorded weddings. There were different volumes for weddings and funerals and First Communions. A modest little archive for St. Hilary's parish. Nowadays much smaller books sufficed for the meager traffic that crossed Father Dowling's desk. No Early-Gardiner wedding had been recorded in the 1947 volume.

"You're sure about the year?"

"I thought I was. It could have been nineteen forty-six."

But it was not recorded in 1946 either. 1948? They might have been engaged in artillery exercises. One long, one short. But they had started on the supposed target.

"How far back do your records go?"

"Nineteen fifteen. I hope you don't want to go through them all."

"I can't believe that I'm mistaken."

"Why do you think the marriage took place here at Saint Hilary's?"

"The family Bible. Oh, it was Saint Hilary's all right."

The parish records were kept in cabinets that ran along one side of the room with bookshelves rising above them. Roger Dowling did not relish the prospect of leafing through more marriage records in search of Paul Gardiner's parents' wedding.

"Your mother was a Catholic?"

"She would have had to be, wouldn't she, in order to . . ." His voice fell away.

"To be married in a Catholic church? Almost certainly, back then. You yourself weren't raised Catholic?"

A lie seemed to rise and set in Gardiner's eyes. "How can you tell?"

"I can't. My housekeeper said you asked for the reverend. If you had said Father . . ."

"Of course. Well, I had no reason to wish to deceive her."

"When did your mother die?"

"A few years ago."

"In the church?"

"Oh. You mean as a Catholic?"

"Yes."

"I don't know."

"Surely you would know something like that."

Gardiner was turning the pages of the ledger as if he might find something Dowling had overlooked.

"You can sit down and go through them all."

"No, Father. Thanks." He closed the ledger. "I've taken enough of your time as it is. I'll check downtown, with the city clerk. He should have a record of the wedding licence."

"I can call down for you, if you'd like."

☆ 13 ☆

"You're too kind. No, I'll go down. If they have a record, I'll want a copy."

"*If* they have a record?"

Gardiner looked rueful. "I'm beginning to doubt my memory, Father Dowling. For all I know, I have the wrong town."

"So Fox River isn't your home?"

"No, it isn't. I really ought to go check the family Bible. I should have come prepared, but I'm doing this on impulse. When I saw the Fox River turn-off I just took it."

"Well, I'm sorry you didn't find what you came for. Perhaps you'll be back."

"Oh no he won't," Marie Murkin said at his elbow. She had come down the hall as he stood at the doorway saying good-by to Paul Gardiner.

"Perhaps not."

"No perhaps about it. What did he want?"

"He was asking about a wedding."

"Was he really?" Mrs. Murkin beamed, her doubts dissipated, and her immediate reassessment of Paul Gardiner was visible on her face. "Who's the girl?"

"That he's going to marry?"

Mrs. Murkin frowned. Roger Dowling did not really regret misleading her. She should not be asking such questions and she knew it. But if Marie Murkin's suspicions of their caller could be lifted by the prospect of a wedding, his own did not go so easily away. Back in his study he picked up the phone and dialed the number of the city clerk. Martin Harrigan assured him that it would be no trouble at all to check on the issuance of a marriage license to a Miss Early and a Mr. Gardiner. The records were all computerized now. Thus it was that, within minutes, Father Dowling knew that no marriage license had been issued to the couple in question in 1947.

"Or any other time in the forties, Father."

"Thank you, Martin."

"You want I should look further?"

"No, I don't think so. Thank you."

He hung up and lit his pipe and contemplated the negative fact that was his. He knew what he did not know. And he did not know if it mattered. Lots of people had not been married in Fox River, or in St. Hilary's parish, in 1947. Was it significant that the parents of Paul Gardiner had not been either?

2

READING Matters, the bookstore Julian Moss and his wife Linda had opened in an old house on Birch Avenue, was more of a hobby than a business. "Just a pastime," each would say, but with considerably different emphasis. Julian had an 8:00 to 5:00 job at the Fox River Savings & Loan and was able to work at the bookstore only evenings and weekends. Linda opened the store every morning at 10:00 and was tied down to it for the rest of the day. Her husband sighed wistfully when he referred to Reading Matters as a pastime, permitting his interlocutor to guess that, if he had his way, the bookstore would be his only job. Of course that would be precarious. They would starve to death if they depended on their income from the sale of books. Indeed, it was doubtful they would make any profit at all if they had not retained a few rooms in the house for their own occupancy, thus making the O'Rourke house their home as well as their place of business.

Julian, tall, stooped, bald, returning to his home and pastime after a day at the Savings & Loan, stood inside the closed door while the warning bell still emitted its tinkle, inhaling with closed eyes the atmosphere of home and of economic independence.

"Just a pastime," Linda echoed. "Some poor women are tied down to their houses, cleaning, washing, ironing, no career, no excitement. Well, I'm tied down to that and also to a houseful of smelly books. I mean it. Just smell. Must, mildew, dust. I live in this atmosphere twenty-four hours a day. Most working women can leave the scene of the crime at the end of the day, but I get to stay right here and cook supper, and at any moment that damned bell can start tinkling and I have another customer ready to spend an hour or more browsing through the stock and then finally maybe buying five or ten dollars' worth of books."

Julian refused to argue with her. They had talked about the store before going into it and Linda had been as enthusiastic as he was. She had always been the more voracious reader of the two of them, devouring paperback thrillers and romances and anything else she could get her hands on. Her reading habits had sometimes seemed obsessive to Julian, almost neurotic. He only wished there were more people like her, now that he was trying to sell books. For the first year, Linda had loved it. The move into the O'Rourke house, being surrounded by all the books, buying and selling, getting to know more and more, speaking with authority. Julian could remember the first time he had overheard Linda discussing Thomas De Quincey with a customer—they had a twelve-volume set, picked up for five dollars in a garage sale. He had not realized how knowledgeable she was. She sold the set for twenty-five dollars. Of course she had developed a little patter about the house too, they both had, and who could blame them if they sounded proprietary when they spoke of Fox River's famous and tragic author?

Linda's attitude had altered when she realized they would not be taking a summer vacation. "We'd better stick close to the store until it's really on its feet," Julian said.

"Let's go away next winter then. To Florida."

They did not go away the next winter either. Julian used his vacation time to buy up more books in the vicinity, traveling to estate sales, garage sales, trinkets-and-treasure sales of women's groups, anywhere that he might come upon unsuspected bargains. They had not had a vacation in two years.

"Who needs a vacation, Julian? The store is our hobby. It's fun! If I get bored, I can always read a book."

She read less now, much less. She had become like a cook with food. Julian did not like the murmur of television coming from their quarters when customers were moving about among the stock. It was like a religious lapse, backsliding, for bookstore owners to listen to television. Linda spent more time than she should in their small and tasteful collection of erotica.

"This is one section everyone looks at."

Julian knew that. He had succumbed to the businessman's temptation: give the customer what he wants. He did not care to think what percentage of the book business could be accounted for by unsavory wares: bogus sexual psychology, marriage manuals, the erotic proper—or improper. His own passion for books was still largely at the prepuberty stage, and no wonder. He had first experienced it when he was a mere boy reading Christopher Morley's *Parnassus on Wheels*. Books, reading, perhaps the dream of writing himself—these had seemed to sum up a better way of being. Such boyhood dreams underlay his ambition to have a bookstore of his own.

Oh, he had been naive, he could admit that to himself and, occasionally, to Linda. He had had mad dreams of holding a kind of court among his books, host to the intelligentsia of the town, having a real author there from time to time. Tea, sherry perhaps, a cultivated atmosphere in which it would be possible to forget that he had spent his day at a desk in the Savings & Loan. That was his mask, his disguise; his real self dwelt among these books in the house that, for a few of his childhood years, had been the home of Francis O'Rourke.

Julian had imagined that something of the *genius loci* would rub off on him. And on Linda too. He would cease being a functionary at the Savings & Loan and Linda . . . What radical alteration in her had he expected? A person less caustic and discontented perhaps, mellower, a bibliophile, a more congenial companion. But Julian could not dismiss the real basis for her complaints. The bookstore was a good deal less than either of them had dreamed.

But this afternoon, when he hurried in at ten after five, expecting the usual muted cry of relief from Linda as she fled to their quarters, free at last of the drudgery of the store, if only free to prepare their evening meal, he was surprised to find her sharing a couch in what had once been the living room of the house with a young man Julian did not know. Linda looked up at her husband with an uncharacteristic warmth in her smile.

"Here's Julian now," she cried. "He knows so much more about the house than I do. Julian, this is . . ." She stopped and her hand lifted apologetically to her mouth.

"Paul Gardiner," the young man said, rising from the couch and extending his hand. "You must be Mr. Moss."

"Yes, I am."

Julian spoke with reserve. Gardiner might well be someone eager to unload an attic full of books and the less he knew of the market the more preposterous would his expectations be. Best to keep a saving distance.

"So Francis O'Rourke lived here," Gardiner said.

Hands in his back pockets, he rotated his torso as if to see the house as it had been.

"From his fourteenth to his nineteenth year."

"Ah."

"Of course the house looked different then."

"No doubt."

"Not completely different, however. I have photographs of the interior as it was at the time. The house has changed far less than the town itself."

"I'm surprised there isn't a commemorative plaque."

"There will be."

"There's the legend on your sign of course."

Sometimes he thought of it as our tainted bookstore's solitary boast, the fact that for those few years of his late youth Frank O'Rourke had lived here, actually moved through these rooms. At the time few suspected what lay ahead of him, but it was Julian's fancy that young O'Rourke himself knew, that the boy had had some intimation of his future. There was some basis for this conjecture in the diary O'Rourke had kept at the time. That diary was the single rare or collector's item Julian Moss possessed, and it was not for sale. He kept it in a glass case in the little sitting area where Linda had been entertaining Paul Gardiner.

"You're interested in O'Rourke?"

"Well, your wife makes him sound very interesting."

Linda said, "I told Mr. Gardiner you might show him the diary."

"I've read a few of the novels, needless to say. As who hasn't?"

Julian attempted a smile. Gardiner's remark suggested that a bookstore was a sure-fire business with multitudes devouring books, at least those of Frank O'Rourke.

"I suppose the diary is very valuable," Gardiner said.

"Yes, it is." How unlike Linda to waste time with someone as illiterate as Gardiner seemed to be. Julian supposed the fellow was good-looking, closer to Linda's age than he himself was. No. Jealousy was absurd and out of the question. Linda sometimes was carried away herself by her little spiel about O'Rourke, and doubtless Gardiner had responded.

"I suppose you're the local expert on O'Rourke," Gardiner said.

"Expert?" Linda said. "Oh, that would be Jim Feehan."

Julian stared at his wife; she had spoken so quickly and with such conviction that it was difficult to imagine there was deliberate malice in her words. But surely she knew of the rivalry between himself and Feehan on the matter of Frank O'Rourke. Feehan was editor of the book page of the local paper, not a full-time job, since there was a book section only on Sundays. His regular job was that of librarian. He headed one of the branch libraries of the Fox River public library system. Feehan had known O'Rourke. At any rate, this was his claim, and it would have been difficult either to corroborate or disprove it. It was a matter of objective fact, on the other hand, that O'Rourke had once lived in the house that now contained Reading Matters. Nor could there be any doubt of the authenticity of the diary in Moss's possession. Feehan might pooh-pooh such provable facts, but they were solid and beyond contest. The librarian's creative memory produced accounts of episodes when he and Frank O'Rourke had fished in the Fox River, had walked home from school together, had vied for the same girlfriend, and on and on. The very banality of these stories convinced most people of their truth and even Julian reluctantly admitted that Feehan must have known Frank O'Rourke when the two of them were young lads in Fox River.

But what really hurt was the recognition that what

Linda had said was true. If one had to consult either Julian Moss or James Feehan on the subject of O'Rourke's fiction, there was little doubt that Feehan was the more knowledgeable, and this had nothing to do with the putative fact that he had known the novelist in his youth. No, Feehan's strength lay in his detailed and exhaustive knowledge of the three novels and the one collection of short stories.

"You should consult Feehan," Julian said to Paul Gardiner, avoiding Linda's eyes as he said it.

Gardiner laughed. "Look, I came in here to buy a book to pass the time in a strange town and the two of you try to turn me into an O'Rourke fan."

"The mysteries are back here," Linda said, leading Gardiner away.

Julian went through the store to their living quarters. The kitchen had been left untouched by the renovations that had turned the house into a bookstore. Frank O'Rourke must have stood at this very window, looking out. But the outer scene had altered beyond recognition. Suddenly it seemed silly to put such value on the fact that an author had spent his youth in this house. It was as silly as Feehan's claim to have walked and talked with Frank O'Rourke.

The claim that really mattered was Feehan's of having in his possession four dozen letters of Frank O'Rourke's.

3

A LIBRARIAN is never seen entering a bar and a newspaperman is seldom seen leaving one. Between the Scylla and Charybdis of these conflicting ideals, Jim Feehan maneuvered his carefully crafted persona that was no stranger to difficult waters. Fox River still bore traces of an earlier time when librarians, like teachers and some others on the public payroll, were expected to be paragons of morality, morality being defined in a generally negative way. Above all: no drinking. But Fox River also honored the equally unrealistic legend that journalists spend the majority of their days in a state of semi-intoxication. When Jim Feehan came into the Foxy Lounge to find Mervel and Ninian ensconced at the bar he was accordingly not surprised.

Mervel looked over a shoulder at his part-time colleague on the *Fox River Messenger*, but Ninian, a stringer for the *Tribune*, contented himself with indirect identification via the mirror behind the bar.

"I'm nearly finished with it," Mervel said apologetically. "I'll have the review for you by Friday."

Feehan nodded. He had forgotten that Mervel was reviewing a book for the page he edited. How long had Mervel had it? Must be months. Hence the guilty look. Feehan did not care whether or not Mervel turned in a review. The book was probably one of those awful novels of the type Mervel himself would dream of writing. Perhaps even now he had a trial page or two in a drawer of his desk. The thought deepened the sour outlook on the world that was Feehan's. He himself was a frequent and caustic reviewer for *The Shopping List*, short devastating dismissals of novels Feehan did little more than flip through. It angered him irrationally that others had the ambition and determination actually to write a book. It smacked of usurpation. He got his own small creative satisfaction damning unread books for *The Shopping List*, a guide flung free at doorsteps in the Fox River valley. The wild surmise about Mervel caused Feehan to take the stool beside Ninian, as if to distance himself from the possibility that anyone as stupid as Mervel might dream of writing a novel.

"What's new said the newsman," Ninian asked. The ice in his glass tinkled a tune trite enough to accompany the remark. Well, it was an improvement over Ninian's standard greeting of a year ago: How's it by you? Feehan had cured Ninian of this insipidity by insisting on taking the question to refer to bayous.

"No, no," Ninian would say with a wounded smile. "By as in by-line. It's German."

"Louisiana was settled by the French. 'Bayou' is a French word."

"Forget it," Ninian said.

"I will if you will."

Ninian got the point, which is more than Mervel would

have done. Feehan had almost convinced Mervel that the Fourth Estate was part of the palace grounds at Versailles.

"I cannot lie said the librarian," Feehan replied to Ninian's amended greeting. "Nothing is new. You are free to be creative."

The bartender waited patiently for Feehan's order. He asked for beer. He wanted something stronger, but beer seemed the wiser course. Ninian said he'd have another himself, perhaps hoping Feehan would pop for it. The hope was dashed.

Mervel said, "I tried to get in touch with Keegan. For some news."

"Try Horvath," Feehan advised. "Keegan is always at the Saint Hilary's rectory boozing it up with the priest."

"Father Dowling doesn't drink," Mervel said. "He quit."

"Good for him. Maybe he can get Keegan to take the pledge too."

The others did not take up this line of talk but Feehan was not really surprised. He himself despised Keegan. The captain of detectives was just a grown-up altar boy, still hanging around priests as if he needed assurance he was doing the right thing. In his reviews for *The Shopping List*, Feehan was particularly hard on any book that seemed to take religious belief seriously.

Having wet his lips with beer, Feehan returned the glass to the bar and contemplated the foam. Bubbles detonating. For some reason, he thought of the brain with its billions of cells, constant commotion, perpetual dying. Entropy. Life is a long slide into nothingness. He drank to that. Not so long a slide in some cases. Poor Frank O'Rourke. Well, he was more famous in death than he had ever been alive. As we are all worth more dead than alive. Insurance. And that goes to the survivors. To Phyllis, Frank's sister, and her poor son of a bitch of a husband, to Jim Feehan, to asses and parasites like Julian Moss. Not to mention the whole tribe of academics who feasted on the remains of the departed novelist. Feehan looked at his watch. 5:15. He had told Paul Gardiner to meet him here at 5:30, thus providing time for a fortifying drink before his arrival. The milder choice of beer had been a second thought. It was important to be on his toes with anyone who came to Fox River wanting to discuss Frank O'Rourke.

When he arrived, Gardiner stood just inside the door of the bar, hands in the pockets of his corduroy sports coat, peering as if into impenetrable dark. Feehan waited for the young man to come to him, grateful for this opportunity to study the impostor. Once accustomed to the mandatory gloom of any place in which spirits are drunk, Gardiner came unerringly to Feehan.

"How did you know which one I would be?"

Gardiner smiled. "I guessed."

"You're from Northwestern?"

Gardiner nodded.

"What department?"

"English," Gardiner said, looking more closely at his questioner. "I'd like a beer myself. Care for another?"

"Why not?"

Feehan had planned to confront Gardiner with the fact that nobody in the English Department at Northwestern had ever heard of him, if the departmental secretary was to be believed. But the man's ineptitude was almost charming. If he were truly devious, he would have used the name of a Northwestern professor. Gardiner tasted his beer and then, having wiped his lips, smiled crookedly at Feehan.

"I'm not at Northwestern, Mr. Feehan. I'm not at any university. I'm just a collector."

"Of O'Rourkiana?"

Gardiner winced at the word, a mark in his favor. "Among other things, yes."

"And you've heard of the letters I have."

"You haven't exactly kept them a secret."

"They're not for sale."

"I didn't imagine they would be. I doubt that I could afford them if they were. I did hope you'd let me have a look at them."

"Maybe even make some Xerox copies?"

"Would you!"

"I certainly would not."

"Julian Moss has offered to let me see the diary."

"Why shouldn't he? There's nothing in it. Portrait of the artist as a very banal boy. You realize that Frank kept that diary when he was fourteen years old."

Gardiner smiled in wonder. "It's strange to hear him referred to so matter-of-factly. Frank. And by someone who knew him."

"His family always called him Francis," Feehan said. Such lies invariably impressed. "Have you been to see Phyllis yet? No? She's part of the tour, you know. And you mustn't forget Keegan."

"Who is Keegan?"

"A cop. Captain of detectives. One of O'Rourke's more improbable friends. Unlike myself."

"I've never heard of Keegan before."

"No reason you should have. I doubt he ever read a word Frank wrote. Maybe he has an anecdote or two, though. It could make your name. What is your real name?"

"Paul Gardiner."

"But not of Northwestern?"

"Chicago. I'm a lawyer."

"I can check on that easily. I checked with Northwestern."

"I'm surprised you had to. I supposed you knew everyone there."

"Well, they know me," he said importantly. "The ones interested in Frank, that is. You might have been a graduate student."

"I'm a little old for that."

"You're kidding."

Gardiner was still conceivably young enough to be working on a dissertation. His neatness told against him, perhaps, no matter his casual dress. Feehan asked him what O'Rourkiana he had managed to collect. This time Gardiner did not wince at the word.

"Some letters to his agent, stolen by a secretary. The galleys of *Where No Storms Come*. There are corrections, though not in O'Rourke's hand. But an editor copied them from a set O'Rourke kept. I don't know who has those."

"Phyllis, probably. She is sitting on a gold mine."

"What does she have?"

Feehan realized that he was impressing Gardiner and it would have been impossible for him not to respond far beyond his knowledge.

"I can only guess. She got everything of a literary sort long before Frank died. The copyrights, of course. They weren't much at the time, but the books sell better every year. That began even before *Purgatorio* was such a success as a film. So she has money, tons of it, and she had all his papers besides." Feehan looked away. "The manuscript of the unpublished novel, all of it."

"You accept the theory of an unpublished novel?"

"It's not a theory. Phyllis has mentioned it." And then, such is the force of habit, he sailed on into the uncharted seas of deception. "I've seen chapters of it."

"What is it about?"

Feehan shook his head. "I don't believe in summarizing novels and this one . . ." His voice drifted reverently away.

"Is it as good as the others?"

Feehan's eyes rested momentarily on Gardiner before turning away. "Better," he said softly. "Infinitely better." His eyes met Gardiner's. "It is unlike anything Frank O'Rourke ever attempted before."

"But what is it about?"

"Love. Death. Beauty. Loss."

Feehan spent the words like coins, dropping them one by one into the vast wishing well his heart had become, sensing their effect on Paul Gardiner, wishing the man were a far vaster audience.

4

FRANK O'Rourke's sister had been called Phyl by her family, a fact that had always seemed vaguely insulting to Phil Keegan, as if it had been aimed at him and all the other Philips in the world.

When they were young and he and Frank would be hanging around the O'Rourke house, the one now turned into a bookstore, maybe sitting on the porch or out back in the huge yard bordered by the largest lilac bushes in town, and Frank said something, calling him Phil, sure enough, Phyllis, if she heard, would answer. Sometimes Frank had meant to address his sister and Keegan felt like an ass when he answered.

"Well, call him Philip," she would say. "In this house, I'm Phyl, not him."

"He."

"Him! Don't be so grammatical."

"If you promise not to be so logical."

She was Frank's older sister, but only by a year or so. That year had meant a lot back then and continued to do so for some time. When she married Emil Mackin, Phyllis seemed to gain several more years on them. Keegan would have thought that, after all these years, with Mackin reduced to a vegetable in a wheelchair and his own wife dead, he would be more at ease with Frank's sister, but he wasn't. Nor did he particularly enjoy his visits to her. He sometimes stopped by on his way to St. Hilary's rectory and an evening of cribbage and conversation with Roger Dowling. In season, when the Cubs were on the road, they would watch the game as they played. The hours spent with his old friend Roger Dowling seemed a reward for his dutiful visit to the sister of his old friend Frank O'Rourke. Phyllis always offered him a drink and he always refused, but that didn't stop her constant sipping on the mixture of Chablis and 7-Up that kept the alcohol level of her blood at a tolerable level of intoxication.

"When did you stop drinking?"

"I didn't. I don't like wine."

"What else would you like?"

"Nothing. My day isn't over."

"You mean you're still on duty?"

Her talk consisted mainly of questions put to Phil Keegan with a noticeable lack of curiosity. She expected no answers, wanted none. She was not interested in him. The questions served only to divert attention from herself and the weird life she led there in the large ranch house overlooking the river, going through the day with a slight buzz on and getting really bombed before she went to bed, which was often at two in the morning or later. God knows, her husband could not be much company for her, slumped in his wheelchair, his bloodshot eyes rolling out of control. Mackin propelled himself through the house, an unguided missile, but he managed to find doorways and miss walls with uncanny accuracy. Phyllis was a small woman, her blonde hair shot with gray now but still reminiscent of the beautiful head of hair that had been her crowning glory way back in grade school. Her face was the puffy one of the drinker, eyes moist, never meeting Keegan's except momentarily. Often he would find her sitting with the drapes pulled, lights on, a jigsaw puzzle on the card table in front of her. It seemed to be the same one she had been working on during his previous visit, and the visit before that. He suspected that she never finished them, just swept them away finally, diverting herself with crossword puzzles until the urge to try another jigsaw came upon her. Language came more easily than shapes. In that she was like Frank, who had been bad even in geometry but had early on shown a fascination with and precocious mastery of language.

"It's an Irish gift, Phil."

"I'm Irish."

"Maybe your family were Vikings."

"You O'Rourkes have blonde hair, we don't. Maybe you're the Vikings."

But it pleased Frank O'Rourke to regard his desire to write as atavistic, an inherited quality.

"*Poetae nascuntur,* Phil."

"Yeah." Everyone else seemed to find Latin easy, but it was the rock on which Phil Keegan's hope to become a priest had broken. He had been at Quigley, the preparatory seminary of the Chicago Archdiocese, in the class behind Roger Dowling, but he simply could not master Latin. A smartass psychiatrist, brought in by the prosecutor, had once suggested to Keegan that his inability to learn Latin had been an expression of his subconscious desire to leave the seminary.

"But I wanted to stay."

"I said subconscious."

"I wanted to but I didn't want to?"

"Not really."

"Bullshit."

Not that he had lived in regret at having failed to become a priest. In the service he had been an MP and after his discharge he got an accelerated trip through the police academy and had been with the Fox River force ever since. He liked his job. Consciously. He didn't give a damn about the subconscious. He doubted that there was any such thing. Roger Dowling seemed to agree with him.

"It's a theoretical convenience, Phil. Like phlogiston."

"Yeah."

"Not that a lot of people aren't vaguely unhappy." Father Dowling touched a match to his pipe and clouds of smoke lifted to the ceiling.

"Psychiatrists think everybody's sick," Keegan groused.

"We are. But not in the way psychiatrists think."

Keegan nodded but said nothing. He supposed the priest meant sin, and that went without saying. Not many people were what they ought to be. God knew Phil Keegan wasn't. When he attended Roger Dowling's noon Mass the prayer that came spontaneously to his lips was that of the penitent. Lord have mercy on me a sinner.

At the time Frank O'Rourke died, Phil Keegan's own wife, God rest her soul, had expressed concern over the novelist's reception in the next world. Frank's life had not been an edifying one, not if you could believe what you read in the paper. He had been more famous than successful; he had had three wives; his days seemed to have turned into a continuous debauch. Whatever the truth of his theory about the Irish and the gift of tongues, Frank O'Rourke had the racial weakness where alcohol was concerned, and that as much as anything else had done him in.

The year before Frank O'Rourke died, Phil Keegan was moved by a newspaper account of the author's losing scuffle with a policeman who had stopped him for driving under the influence. Phil wrote to his old friend. He got the address from Phyllis, wrote Frank and told him to come home to Fox River. He didn't say it right out, but what he wanted to convey was the thought that in his home town any misunderstandings Frank might have with the law would not become items in the national news. California was an unnatural environment. Frank needed the stabilizing atmosphere of the Midwest.

Frank's answering letter, typed, was unlike any Keegan had ever seen. Frank used the typewriter in such a way that the mechanical was dominated by the personal. He disdained capitals and ordinary punctuation, letting series of dots and asterisks serve as signals for the units of composition, which were not sentences. Phrases. The beginnings of a thought, suggestions. "Inchoative" was the word Frank himself would have used. Phyllis did use it when Keegan mentioned her brother's reply to his invitation to come home.

The burden of the reply was that Frank O'Rourke carried with him all the Fox River he needed.

> Fx is 1 rvr into which i cn alwys step
> twice (*pace* Harry Cletus) . . . it runs in me
> still . . . still waters run deep . . . my time
> there is my litry capital . . . the banks of
> the Fx Rvr . . . of cos mine aint yrs . . . there
> where you do your coptivating is an
> impersonadir . . . thanx anyway always . . .

In more standard English, he suggested that since Keegan was such a big muckamuck now he should make Frank O'Rourke an honorary chief so that he could confront his adversaries on the local constabulary on a more equal footing. And he asked if Keegan remembered Captain Midnight and hikometers.

"Imagine him remembering that," Keegan said to Phyllis.

"It's a writer's capital, his memory. That's what he's saying in the letter. Are you going to keep it?"

"Do you want it?"

"Dear God, I have enough letters and memorabilia of the immortal Francis O'Rourke. I mean, you should keep it. His letters will be collectors' items one day."

He might have dismissed it as the pardonable pride of an older sister, except that Phyllis had never been all that impressed by Frank. In any case, Keegan found the thought that a friend of his could be the object of that kind of interest crazy. Frank was notorious, that was clear enough, he was something of a celebrity of the scandalous sort. But famous? Famous for what? For writing stories?

Phil Keegan found it difficult to think of telling stories as a fully adult occupation. It seemed a prolongation of childhood and that fitted in with Frank's behavior. He had never really grown up. Three wives? How could you take someone who had had three wives seriously? And who told stories. Makebelieve. Keegan had never read any of Frank's stories. He had seen the movie though and hadn't much cared for it. It had been an odd mixture of the dreamy and the violent, unreal. Phil Keegan did not see many more movies than he read books. His idea of recreation was watching the Cubs play in Wrigley Field.

"A boys' game," Phyllis had murmured, sipping her wine and 7-Up.

"Not the way the Cubs play it," Keegan said loyally, but it was a wasted remark. Had Phyllis ever been to a ball game?

"I suppose I must have been. Didn't you and Frank play?"

"I did."

"Didn't Frank?"

Keegan suppressed a smile. Sometimes they had put Frank O'Rourke in right field and prayed that no grounders got past the first baseman. Frank was a natural nonathlete. The funny thing was that, according to Phyllis, sports figured prominently in his stories.

"As a metaphor, of course."

Keegan lit a cigar without apology. A ball game was a ball game as far as he was concerned.

"There are always collectors in town," Phyl said, moving pieces of her puzzle about on the card table. "I won't see them."

"Collectors of what?"

"Of things concerning Frank. Letters, manuscripts, anything. Do you know that a bookstore in town actually has a diary of Frank's on display? Think of it. A private diary. Where did they get it? It's indecent. They wouldn't leave him alone when he was alive and now that he's dead it's worse."

"Are you saying the diary was stolen?"

"Of course it wasn't stolen."

"How could someone get hold of Frank's diary . . ."

"Oh, he probably gave it to someone who sold it to a dealer who auctioned it off."

"Why would anyone want his diary?"

"What have I been telling you, Phil Keegan? They want anything and everything. And not just things. Memories. They collect other people's memories on tape. I'm surprised they haven't bothered you."

"You ought to have someone here with you, Phyllis."

"My God, I'm tripping over people as it is."

Her husband, nutty as a fruitcake, moving about the house in his motorized wheelchair? Her cook, who was fruity in another way? The yardman?

Keegan said, "I worry about you."

"Don't. Have a drink instead."

"That's one reason I worry, your drinking."

Phyllis applied the whooshing flame of a butane lighter to her cigarette and squinted at him through clouds of exhaled smoke. He wished she wouldn't smoke either. But she seemed fated to drown in booze or be consumed by fire. He wondered if even Roger Dowling could make a dent in her protective armor.

"She may be a drinker, Phil, but she sounds protected from the usual consequences of it. A person has to be brought low before they can come out of it. She may seem helpless to you, but in her own mind she is still in full control. She runs that house, after all. She has to lose the sense of being in control of her life before I could be of any help to her."

Keegan nodded. Lately he seemed to be getting a lot of theory from everybody. Of course he was used to it from Roger Dowling. And he could accept it from his old friend. Priests are supposed to be savvy about the human heart. It's their job. It wasn't just a matter of private talent, a knack.

"Roger, do you realize people are collecting anything having to do with her brother? Letters, manuscripts, anything."

"I'm not surprised. Relics."

Keegan was a little shocked that Roger Dowling should compare the letters and papers of Frank O'Rourke with the relics of the saints. But he was reminded of his late wife's uncharacteristic remark when Frank died, and felt ashamed.

"Well, I took Phyllis's advice and kept the letter he wrote me."

"God loves the unlettered too, Phil."

"Yeah. We going to watch the Cubs or not?"

5

THE FOLLOWING morning, Roger Dowling read his breviary while walking back and forth on the sidewalk connecting the rectory and the sacristy door of St. Hilary's church. Psalms, hymns, selections from the gospels and the Fathers of the Church, the breviary was a florilegium, an anthology, of Christian lore. Roger Dowling thought of it as designed with an eye to the man wanting one book with him on that legendary desert island. But it was a book of four volumes, one per season. Roger still read the *Breviarium Romanum* in Latin although there were English versions now, just as the liturgy too was in the vernacular. Well, Roger Dowling would say his Mass in English, but the breviary was a prayer he prayed in solitude and saying it in Latin needed no excuse.

His favorite books, like the breviary, were libraries unto themselves: the *Summa theologiae* of Aquinas, the *Divina commedia* of Dante. He would truly settle for those three books alone. The one book he hoped never to read again was the *Code of Canon Law*.

Roger Dowling had spent the better part of his priestly career as a member of the marriage court of the Archdiocese of Chicago. He had been a specialist in failure, a daily dealer in heartbreak and the impossibly tangled webs woven when men and women practise to deceive. Abandoned wives pleaded for annulments, men who claimed their spouses withheld their bodies and all affection asked to be dealt a new hand in the game of life. The claimant was always innocent, the accused partner black with guilt. It could not really be like that. How often the abandoned wife was an accomplice in the flight and the unloved husband deliberately unlovable, demanding affection with a snarl. How many husbands and wives seemed to keep score.

The guilty party is each of us. No man is without sin. No court, no code of law, can undo the past, make what we have done as if it had never been. We are what we have done. A new self can be created only by a prolonged sequence of deeds, not by a ruling, not by a judgment that events which occurred never really happened. Such basic truths as these were burned into Roger Dowling's consciousness.

Yet it was impossible not to share the mad hopes of the majority of those who came before the court. There was not a chance in the world that their marriages would be annulled, but the flaring hope for a new beginning, the unfounded belief that, in a different setting, untrammeled by past promises, one would be a completely altered person, capable of nobility, even heroism, was contagious. Understanding that dream, knowing it was doomed, not wanting to thwart hope precipitously yet fearful of raising false expectations, Roger Dowling led a life of participated anguish. He began to drink. For some years he drank secretly and without any public manifestation or impairment of his duties. As a member of the marriage court, as one with a doctorate in canon law, he was one of those from whose ranks new bishops are named. He had every right to expect that he was meant for higher things. Certainly others thought so. But the drinking grew worse and then it did interfere and he had his first blackout—a period of time, nearly a full day, of which he had no clear memories whatever.

He took the cure in Wisconsin at a place that specialized in clerical alcoholics. Alcoholics. Ah, the power of words. On Molokai, after years of ministering to the lepers, Father Damien began his sermon one Sunday with the words, "We lepers. . . ." So Roger Dowling had had to learn to say, "We alcoholics. . . ." It had meant the end of any thought of ecclesiastical advancement. Somewhat to his own surprise, Roger Dowling was relieved by this knowledge, and when he was offered St. Hilary's Parish in Fox River, Illinois, a town west of Chicago, he was glad to accept. To others his assignment might represent the end of the line, the Ultima Thule of the Archdiocese of Chicago, but to Roger Dowling it increasingly was home, the definition of peace. It was true the parish had seen better days; true, too, that it was in a state of decline. The parish school was closed; there simply were not enough children to warrant keeping it open. But it had become a parish social center that catered to the disproportionate numbers of elderly people in the parish.

And there was Phil Keegan, the man he had known as a boy in Quigley, though in truth Roger Dowling's memories of the young Phil Keegan were dim. Keegan, being in the class behind, would have sharper memories. One's glance went forward in school, to upperclassmen, the approaching goal. Keegan had dropped out of the seminary, as so many do. Yet here they were, together in Fox River. Keegan stopped by the rectory often and

Roger Dowling encouraged his visits. The captain of detectives confided in him, and the priest had more than once become involved in cases under investigation. Phil Keegan, he had come to think, was the representative of justice, while his own role was to represent mercy. Police are concerned with crime, but the priest is concerned with sin. And sins can be forgiven.

"Then a lot of judges think they're priests," Keegan growled. "They love to forgive and forget."

But grumble as he might, Phil Keegan loved his work. Oh, he might sit around the rectory and urge Roger Dowling to remember the good old days in the seminary, over thirty years ago, but Phil must realize he was well out of the priesthood. It had not been his vocation. Roger Dowling thought painfully of all the priests and nuns who had left over the past decade, for reasons he found at best obscure. Better to have left before ordination or profession, as Phil Keegan had. Phil was meant to be a cop, just as Roger Dowling, whatever his failings, was thoroughly a priest. After all, how could one be a dispenser of mercy if he did not realize his own need of it? Roger Dowling was not happy about all the changes in Holy Mother Church, but he had no doubt that she would muddle through.

Now, reading his breviary, Roger Dowling stopped in a patch of shade thrown by a mountain ash that flanked the walk. He closed his book on his finger and listened to the melodic call of a cardinal. Keegan had irked him last night and Roger Dowling was now ashamed of his impatience.

It was while they had been speaking of Mrs. Mackin, Phyllis Mackin, whom Phil constantly referred to as Frank O'Rourke's sister.

"The writer," Keegan explained. "He wrote a lot of books."

"I know."

"Have you read them?"

"Some of them."

"He was raised here in Fox River. I knew him."

"Have you read his books, Phil?"

"I saw a movie based on one of them. It was okay. He had a great reputation, though, and he made a lot of money. That all went to Phyllis, I suppose. Some of it did. She got a lot anyway. Not that it does her much good."

"What's wrong?"

"Her husband." Keegan twirled a finger around his ear. "We used to pick him up in the park, at four in the morning, just sitting there on a bench with a dull look on his face. Not drunk or anything. Phyllis never even knew he was out of the house until we brought him home."

"Where is he now?"

"At home. Finally he really flipped, can't talk, drools a lot, pretty sad. But he can get around in a wheelchair so Phyllis keeps him with her."

Roger Dowling thought of that marriage. It was a sharp reminder of the old days. How often the spouse of a committed mental patient or of someone who had a stroke came, wanting release from the marriage bond.

"How is the wife doing?"

"She drinks."

"Eventually she'll end up gaga, like her husband."

"Maybe. Maybe not. Roger, you should talk with her." Phil said this as if it were an inspiration, and it was the expression on his face rather than the words that irked Roger Dowling. One drunk to another? Phil hadn't said that but his expression did.

"If she wants to talk to me, of course I'll see her."

"I'll give you the address."

"Have her come here."

He said it sharply, but Phil did not seem to notice.

"I'll try. I could just bring her along for a visit. You know, come meet my old friend Roger Dowling. Once she gets used to you, you'll be able to get through to her. I'm sure of it."

Again the unexpressed thought seemed to be that if Roger Dowling could conquer drink, anyone could. Why should he find this thought annoying? But it was one thing to admit his weakness to himself and another to be reminded of it by someone else. Fortunately a flurry of activity on the television screen had drawn Phil's attention back to the Cub game. He had not mentioned Mrs. Mackin again until he was leaving.

"I'll bring her along some night soon, all right?"

"Of course."

Bothered by these memories, Roger Dowling tried to resume the reading of his breviary, but he could concentrate only imperfectly. He must assume that Phil Keegan hadn't noticed and been offended by his curtness. Even worse, he had acted inexcusably to a clear appeal to his role of priest. If he could be of some help to the Mackin woman, he had no right to refuse.

Roger Dowling began to walk toward the rectory. He would telephone Phil and get the Mackin woman's address and phone number. Once he had those, he would think of some plausible excuse for dropping by and talking with her.

6

THE SUN bright on the drawn shades illumined the lace curtains of Doris Hagstrom's bedroom, but Doris, seated at her electric typewriter, did not notice. Her eyes were closed, her head cocked, as if she were attending to the hum of the machine. She was, but this was not distraction. Something like inspiration seemed to be occurring. The noise of the typewriter had put her in mind of the electric clock in the family room downstairs, the irritating buzz of which seemed an accompaniment to her dissatisfying life. That clock had been a wedding present. How many wedding presents did they still have? Right after the wedding they had gone off by train to Canada, leaving most of their wedding gifts stashed in the attic at Henry's mother's house. The clock had gone with them, running on Canadian current for two years and then on various other power sources before they had settled down here in Fox River.

That buzzing electric clock seemed a metaphor of sorts, perhaps a symbol of their lives, drawing sustenance from different environments, eliciting their complaints. Doris opened her eyes. The thought was elusive. For a moment, it had seemed—what? Doris looked at her machine in sudden anger, then switched it off and pushed away from her desk.

She wore a housecoat. The kids were at school, Henry was at work, she was at home. Most of her friends had jobs, but she did not want one. Oh, it all sounded nice, independence, money of her own, meeting new people. But Doris could not kid herself that it would be anything other than a grind doing the kind of work she was likely to get. Not that she wasn't ambitious. She wanted to write. It was her dream—to write, to be published, to be known as an author. She pressed the back of her hand against her forehead and tried to surprise herself in the mirror, seeing herself before she saw herself seeing herself.

She knew exactly the kind of picture of herself she wanted on the dust jacket of her first book. If she ever wrote a book. The truth was that she had trouble writing even short things and she had never had anything published. Yet. Yet! She was forty-two years old and she had dreamed of being an author ever since she was in college. An author. A writer. She had not been clear what it was she wanted to write and indeed, in the years since college, in a desultory fashion, she had attempted poetry, articles, humor, short stories, and a novel. At the outset, she thought of herself as Jane Austen. Now she would settle for Erma Bombeck. She had never actually begun to write the novel, but she had a shoe box filled with index cards: notes on characters, aspects of the plot, sketches of settings, on and on, hours of preliminary work that had proved to be prelude to nothing else. She had decided she was not meant to be a novelist.

"There are too damn many books already," Henry

would say, and she knew he was trying to cheer her up. He was willing to read anything of hers she gave him and invariably he praised what she had done. "This is really good, honey!"

"It needs work."

"I don't see where."

"You're too easily pleased."

"Like hell I am. What are you going to do with this?"

"It's not finished."

"You should send it to the *Fox River Messenger*, for the Op Ed page."

Once she would have sneered at such a goal, but she had followed Henry's suggestion and sent several items to the editor of the *Messenger*. They all came back. Doris was heartbroken. She had imagined the whole town poring over her words, she had imagined strangers stopping her in the street, wanting to tell her how much they enjoyed what she had written. And then she got the lovely note from James Feehan, the first real encouragement she had received. On the basis of her meeting with Jim, she had as much as told Agnes Florey that something of hers was going to be published.

"Where?"

"I want it to be a surprise."

"You tell me about it and want it to be a surprise? Don't be silly. Where are you going to be published?"

"Well, maybe it's a little grand to speak of it as being published. It's only the newspaper."

"The *Tribune*!"

"No. The *Messenger*."

Agnes acted as though appearing in the *Messenger* was nothing at all, yet Doris had good reason to suspect that her friend and fellow aspiring writer had been trying as diligently as she to get something into the *Messenger*.

"I'm working on a short story," Agnes had said. She

was a wiry woman who had never carried an extra pound except during her two pregnancies. She ate anything and everything without noticeable effect on her weight. It was not fair. Doris had to watch her diet as if she were a bundle of allergies. Calories were her allergy. If she smelled something cooking, she gained weight. It was a species of heroism to keep her weight at 140. Thank God, she was tall, nearly five eight. Jim Feehan said men did not like meatless women.

The ringing telephone snapped her from her reverie. Involuntarily her heart leaped with hope, as if she had something being considered by the *Messenger* and it might be Jim Feehan on business for a change. But it was Agnes.

"I hope I'm not disturbing you while you're writing, Doris."

"I've finished my stint."

"So have I. Coffee?"

"If you come here."

Agnes agreed. She lived only two doors away. Doris did not feel bad about lying to Agnes. The few sentences she had written about the buzzing clock could scarcely be called a stint. But she suspected that Agnes too put the best possible face on her own writing efforts. She decided to tell Agnes that the *Messenger* was not going to publish anything of hers.

"Oh, no," Agnes cried, and her distress seemed genuine. "You too?"

"Did you send something to the *Messenger*?" Doris peered at her friend, wondering how much they might have in common beyond their literary ambitions.

"No. The *Ladies Home Journal*. It came back today."

"A letter?"

"A printed rejection slip."

The two women sat at the kitchen table, crouched over their cups of coffee, book ends of despondency.

"What was your piece about?" Agnes asked.

"My impressions of the Fox River."

"Uh huh."

"I thought, local paper, local color." But all she had gotten was Jim Feehan's unsolicited memories of his youth, more stories about Frank O'Rourke.

Agnes shrugged, conceding the logic. "But who cares about the Fox River?"

"It's the name of the town."

"I know. So why rub it in?"

Agnes and Bill Florey had moved to Illinois from Connecticut and she tended to speak of their life in the Midwest as if it were a Babylonian captivity.

"I've switched to biography," Doris said.

"No kidding. Whose?"

Her conversations with Agnes seemed a tissue of lies. She said unblinkingly, "Frank O'Rourke's." It just came out, prompted perhaps by thoughts of Jim Feehan.

"He's been worked to death."

"Not the local angle."

"Don't forget, Doris, he got out of here as soon as he could. What do you have in mind, a piece for the *Messenger*?"

"I may be able to use parts of it that way."

"Parts of it? Are you thinking of a book?"

"It could end up book-length, yes."

Agnes, despite herself, was impressed. But she had been impressed by Doris's shoe box full of embryo novel. Was this the extent of the fame Doris was meant to enjoy, telling lies to Agnes Florey? Agnes wanted to know how she was going about it, and the question released a flow of words that made Doris herself marvel. Fiction should be easy as pie for her, the way she could go on like this over coffee with Agnes. She spoke of interviews, of digging at the county clerk's office, of long visits to the O'Rourke home.

"You mean Reading Matters?"

"Yes. Of course the O'Rourkes lived in other houses too."

Agnes slapped a palm on the table and shook her head. "Damn. Why didn't I think of that? What a dope I am!"

"I hope no one else thinks of it." Doris was so gratified by Agnes's reaction that she thought she really would try to write something about Frank O'Rourke, the Fox River novelist.

"Don't you realize that Bill is Frank O'Rourke's sister's lawyer?"

"You're kidding!"

"I am not. Phyllis O'Rourke Mackin. I met her myself once, for heaven's sake, on her annual trip to the office. She's a very shy woman."

"Could Bill get me an introduction?"

Agnes sat back in her chair. Eyes downcast, she ran a finger around the rim of her coffee mug. "Doris, how far along in the O'Rourke manuscript are you?"

"Why?"

Agnes's eyes lifted. "Doris, we could collaborate! Lots of people do it. We could write the thing together."

"Or I don't get to meet Frank O'Rourke's sister?"

"Don't look at it like that. Wouldn't it be a change, writing with someone? And Doris, it's a great idea. Fox River, Frank O'Rourke. Sure, lots of things have been written on him, but most of it is either very scholarly or just gossipy, concentrating on the disintegration in California. We can focus on the years of promise, the years of hope. The home town of Frank O'Rourke." Agnes pronounced the final sentence as if it were a title.

"There must be lots of people who still remember him. We can use a tape recorder."

And so the two friends, no longer rivals, fell to planning the campaign for their joint endeavor. Agnes was not even bothered when Doris confessed that she hadn't really drafted anything yet, she was still in the note-taking stage.

They drank a fourth cup of coffee. They had another cigarette too. Agnes began to think aloud, wondering how they could use her husband in order to get close to Phyllis O'Rourke Mackin.

"She drinks," Agnes said knowingly.

"Good," Doris replied.

They clicked their mugs in a toast, collaborators, conspirators, aspiring authors.

Doris had as well the odd thought that she had hit upon a way to get back at Jim Feehan.

7

WHEN Bill Florey went west he was no longer a young man, but
of course if he had been much younger he would not have had
the peculiar professional competence that Fish, Fleischer and
Finn had wanted him for. He had suggested that quarterly con-
sultations would suffice, but he was merely being coy. From the
moment the offer was broached, Fox River, Illinois, had seemed
the doorway out of the closed room of his life. His professional
life.

It was really not surprising that Fish, Fleischer and Finn
should have regarded his somewhat standard experience in
the Manhattan literary world as a precious and rare expertise.
In a sense it was. Yes, it certainly was. Why could he never consider what he did as important? It was as if his imagined real self
had been developing somewhere else and was waiting for him to
join up. Some idyllic dream of a Midwestern suburban lawyer

got him in its grip and, in the end, he had succumbed to the temptation Fish, Fleischer and Finn put before him. Perhaps they wanted him because his name began with an F. In any case, he would become a partner and take on the task of managing the affairs of Mrs. Phyllis Mackin.

"The name will mean nothing to you," Fleischer had said. They were having drinks in the Century Club. Fleischer was suitably impressed by these surroundings. Indeed, it was only with a visible effort that the Illinois lawyer resisted identifying the notables who drifted by where they sat in chairs at the head of the stairs. Soon, after Bill Florey had had his mandatory two martinis, they would go in to lunch. "The name Frank O'Rourke will."

Bill Florey widened his eyes, to indicate that the name Frank O'Rourke did indeed mean something to him. The author, whose personal bad luck had been his literary good luck, had committed suicide the year before, disappearing as Ambrose Bierce and B. Traven had before him, with the signal difference that O'Rourke had left a suicide note.

"She is his sister and has in her possession all his papers. He turned everything literary over to her."

"Wasn't O'Rourke married?"

"Several times."

"Well?"

"The first wife died years ago. The second wife remarried and wants to hear nothing of her late and unlamented husband. The third is a nurse turned addict."

"Children?"

"Two sons by the first wife."

"Surely they were mentioned in the will?"

"They were. Trust funds. They are not much, but given the profligacy of O'Rourke's life, the wonder is that he thought to provide for them at all. The point is that all his literary property, copyrights, royalties, papers, letters, etcetera, etcetera, were turned over to his sister Phyllis before his death. Our client, Mrs. Mackin, that is. No one in the firm has sufficient experience with this sort of property to feel confident in the matter. We need someone with experience in literary property."

Bill Florey sipped his second martini, wondering what sort of information Fleischer had gathered about his career. Experience in literary property. He was almost surprised to realize how accurately that phrase described his professional life. But Fleischer would see in it a glamour no longer visible to Bill Florey.

"You don't want to take me just to look after one client?" That was when he suggested acting as consultant to the firm. He had not wanted Fleischer to agree. Had it been a last half-conscious attempt to hang on to the security he had? But Fleischer persisted. Of course they would expect Mr. Florey to do more than handle Mrs. Mackin's affairs. "Though they may prove to be more extensive than you imagine."

In that certainly Fleischer had been right, the amateur seeing what the expert had not. Bill Florey should have known that Frank O'Rourke's reputation was on the rise and that his literary remains would soon become a small industry. In the event, Bill Florey became a lawyer with a single client. He was as close as he had ever been to contentment. He loved Fox River. It was a decent place in which to raise children. Agnes spoke with increasingly forced nostalgia of the East, but it had been several years now since they had even been back for a visit. Their parents were dead and neither Agnes nor Bill had ever been close to brothers and sisters. They had become Midwesterners.

And that, as Frank O'Rourke had written, is a moral condition, not merely a geographical designation. Strangers descending on Chicago in summer were surprised to find that the huge metropolis was all but concealed beneath great green clouds of trees. Only along the lake front itself did the profile of the city thrust upward and even there Lake Shore Drive wended among acres of parks and boulevards. If legendary Chicago turned out to be pastoral, the suburbs and the cities to the west were even more so. Fox River struck Bill Florey as mythical, fictive, the stuff of novels. And so it had been for Frank O'Rourke.

Bill got along with Phyllis Mackin because he was glad to drink with her.

"Martini," he had said on his first visit when she asked him at ten in the morning what he would have to drink. He had not hesitated. He had already noticed her glass on the card table when he entered the room. Her smile was one of complicity. Kindred spirits.

By the time the cook minced in with a pitcher of martinis, Bill Florey and Phyllis O'Rourke Mackin were at ease with each other. It was a pleasure to both of them to drink at that hour of the day without apology.

"Never trust a man who doesn't drink. My father told us that."

"Did he drink?"

"In moderation."

"Unlike his son Frank?"

"And unlike his daughter Phyllis."

They drank to that, or seemed to. If anything, she had more confidence in Bill Florey than did Fish, Fleischer and Finn.

"There seems good reason to believe that my brother's things are, well, valuable."

It was the wildest of understatements. Florey renewed some copyrights, checked the contracts O'Rourke had signed. Dear God, how publishers had once robbed authors. Of course there was an element of risk in bringing out the first novel, but provisos could have been written into the contract. Nowadays they almost certainly would be. O'Rourke had not even saved all his contracts and it had been necessary for Florey to request copies. Soon he had the O'Rourke properties producing a maximum yield. He himself became fascinated with the possibilities. Fish, Fleischer and Finn were delighted they had brought him into the firm, as well they might be. If he had one regret it was that he could not convince Phyllis that her brother's unfinished novel ought to be published. She was simply irrational on the subject. Having showed it to him, she stashed it away and would not let him see it again. Was she worried that it wasn't good enough? It wouldn't matter. The thing would sell like crazy even if it were gibberish, because it was Frank O'Rourke gibberish. But Phyllis could not have been concerned for her brother's literary reputation. Had it really surprised him to learn that she did not care in the least for his fiction?

"I loathe it. I've never finished one of the novels and none of his short stories is short enough for me. Do I shock you?"

He would not have admitted it if she had. What did surprise him was the attraction he felt for her. He was nearly a decade younger than she was. She had not taken care of herself. She drank from dawn to dusk, or whatever their terminal equivalents were in the crazy day she lived. It was true that there were reminders of a lost beauty in her. The teary eyes had once been sharp and dazzling blue; beneath the puffiness, smooth creamy skin that once had been, signaled its still latent presence. But, most of all, he was comfortable with her. When he arrived at midmorning for a conference, she received him as often as not in her bedroom.

Her coquettish manner should have been repellent. She was too old for such nonsense; it ought to have seemed grotesque. Somehow it did not. Somehow one thing led to another. The first time, afterward, she wept and he might have been annoyed if he had not just then heard from afar the whirr of her husband's wheelchair.

"How long has he been like that?"

She had not wanted to talk about it and Florey got the story from Finn. "He was some kind of a pervert. The police arrested him several times, sitting in the park with nothing on at three or four in the morning. His clothes were in a neat pile on the bench beside him."

"He looks as though he's had a stroke."

"That's right."

"Is his mind clear?"

"Damned if I know. People like that make me nervous."

Bill Florey thought of the drooling man, head lolling, unable to focus his eyes, pointlessly moving about the house in a motorized wheelchair. What would the poor fool make of it if he came upon his wife in bed with her lawyer?

Bill Florey told himself that he would be better advised to worry about the cook. Or even the yardman.

And Agnes.

But Agnes noticed nothing. They made love so seldom now that each time should have been an event. But he would not have been startled if Agnes ate an apple and went on reading her book while he sweated to his solitary climax.

"Doris and I are going to collaborate," Agnes said, after squirming out from beneath him and switching on the light beside the bed.

"Good."

"We need your help."

"Bad."

"Now Bill, when did I ever ask you for a favor? As far as my writing is concerned, I mean."

Her writing? She had been taking courses in writing for

as long as he could remember. At the Y, at the library, through the mail. She talked incessantly about her writing. Yet she wrote little. Once he was certain that she meant it when she said she did not want him reading what she wrote, it was safe to insist.

"I do know a thing or two about writing, Agnes."

It was odd, trying to impress his wife, but Agnes had not paid much attention when he sketched for her what he had managed to do with the writings of Frank O'Rourke. He doubted she had heard a word he said. Until she asked him for the favor.

"All we want to do is interview her."

"No."

"Don't say no. Let her decide."

"I am telling you her decision. She does not want to talk about her brother Frank."

"She told you that?"

"I am her lawyer. I represent her in handling what her brother wrote. I know how she feels about it."

"What exactly did she say?"

Bob Florey smiled. The spectacle of Agnes attempting to be cunning was ridiculous. It was ridiculous too to treat her request as if it were serious. She had not written anything yet and she was unlikely to start now. Had her friend Doris written anything? He could not remember.

"Will you be content with what I tell you?" he asked Agnes.

"It would be better if we talked to her."

"That's out of the question."

She snuggled closer. "Okay. You tell me. First of all, what is she like?"

He felt a bit like a writer himself, describing Phyllis. The portrait of a bedridden arthritic woman who did not let a month go by without rereading at least one of her beloved brother's books had nothing to do with Phyllis Mackin, but Agnes seemed to find it plausible.

"Isn't she married?"

"Her husband had a stroke."

"How old is she?"

He hesitated. "About our age."

"The poor thing," Agnes said, cuddling closer still. "Her devotion to her brother must be some sort of . . ."

"Compensation?"

"Yes."

"You may be right."

"Why are you smiling?"

For answer, he squeezed her. Agnes accepted it. She turned off the light again. Bill Florey fell asleep to the steady sound of Agnes telling him of the really great book she and Doris were going to write.

8

PAUL Gardiner phoned again and again and Jim Feehan was increasingly uneasy. By his own admission, young Gardiner had lied about an academic affiliation with Northwestern; he had also lied when he claimed to be a Chicago lawyer. Both lies were so easily detected that Feehan had to assume Gardiner meant them to be, at least by anyone with the least bit of curiosity. Jim Feehan did not consider his curiosity to be the least. Attempting to put Doris Hagstrom on to Gardiner had been a forlorn hope.

"I want to meet people who can *give* me information about Frank O'Rourke. More importantly, I want to have a long talk with you."

"You're writing something?"

"Yes!" She said it with a little squeal of excitement and for a moment Feehan hated her. Were his own ambitions to be so cruelly mocked? First the absurd fear that Mervel might write a novel and now Doris Hagstrom, for the love of God, announcing that she and Agnes Florey were teaming up on a book about Frank O'Rourke. "The writer from the local angle. We'll use lots of photographs, everything."

"Talk to Gardiner."

"Why? Who is he?"

"That is the question, my love. I want to find out who he is."

"Then ask him."

Feehan smiled. Dear Doris. But it was he who was ridiculous, thinking that she could be pressed into service to find out who Paul Gardiner was and what he was really up to. Such a task required an expert.

"Do you have a photo of the subject?" Tuttle asked importantly. When he tipped back in his chair, his hat, an Irish tweed, tipped over his eyes. Feehan wondered if the little lawyer smoked a pipe as well.

"Why do you ask?"

"I don't trust people who smoke pipes."

"Hmmm."

"You smoke one?"

"I don't smoke anything, Mr. Feehan, but if I did, that would be my business. Is that what you have against Gardiner, that he smokes?"

"He doesn't smoke."

"What else do you know about him?"

"That he doesn't teach at Northwestern, that he is not a Chicago lawyer."

"Is he some other kind of lawyer?"

"You'd be a better judge of that than I would."

Tuttle, who had been taking notes, nodded. His office was not impressive. Neither was he. Feehan wondered if Mervel and Ninian were playing a joke on him, giving him Tuttle's name when asked advice about a discreet investigator.

"Tuttle knows everything," Mervel said.

"He has done some amazing things," Ninian agreed.

"I never heard of a lawyer acting as a private detective."

"Tuttle will do anything once."

"Do you do this sort of thing often?" Feehan asked Tuttle.

Tuttle considered the question with narrowed eyes. He had removed his hat. His startled hair did not instill any more confidence than had the now removed hat. "Much of what a lawyer does is dig, Mr. Feehan. Knowledge." Tuttle tapped his head audibly. "You have to know more than the opposition. No surprises." Tuttle's brows went up as presumably they would if he were ever to be surprised.

"I won't pretend that I'm consulting you on somebody else's behalf, Mr. Tuttle."

Tuttle nodded. "Good."

"Paul Gardiner first showed up in Fox River a week ago. He contacted me. He got in touch with the Mosses at Reading Matters."

"I beg your pardon?"

"It's a bookstore. The Mosses run it. It is located in a house once occupied by the O'Rourke family. Frank O'Rourke lived there."

"I see."

"You do know who Frank O'Rourke is?"

"Just tell me in your own words."

Well, Tuttle might have pretended he knew, and that would have wasted more time. Feehan started at the beginning and finally returned to the topic of Paul Gardiner.

Tuttle scratched his head with the sharp end of his

pencil. "I must have missed something. What is it that you think Gardiner wants?"

"I don't know. I've explained the value of . . . "

"You think he's after the O'Rourke letters you have?"

"He could be."

"Has he expressed interest in them?"

"Yes."

Tuttle frowned. "If he were going to steal them, or any of the other things you mentioned, why would he make himself known to so many people and express interest in O'Rourke papers and letters and the like?"

"That's what bothers me."

"He hasn't broken any laws."

Feehan let out air. "If he had broken laws I would have gone to the police, Mr. Tuttle. What I want is information. Knowledge." Feehan tapped his head but was unable to elicit the hollow thump that Tuttle had.

"First we'll find out if he has a record."

"I don't want the police in on this."

Tuttle winked. "Don't worry. I've got connections. You have the letters with you?"

He did. His thought was to put them in a safe-deposit box at the bank, out of harm's way. Tuttle vetoed that.

"There they would be inaccessible nights, weekends, holidays."

"I want them safe."

"Where better than in a safe?" Tuttle moved a picture on the wall to reveal the door of a safe. "Where better than right here?"

Feehan left the letters and then the lawyer's office with the conviction that Tuttle had a fool for a client. It was preposterous to confide, even to a lawyer, the unease he felt whenever a

Frank O'Rourke fan came to Fox River. The very ingenuousness of Paul Gardiner seemed a subtle threat. Feehan stopped at a drugstore and bought a package of cigarettes, the filter of which made up two-thirds the length. Back in his car, he lit one and inhaled. Nothing. He made sure the thing was lit. It was. Again he attempted to inhale. This brand would cause hernia before it harmed the lungs. Feehan sniffed the smoke fresh off the tip of the cigarette. It had a medicinal-laboratory odor. Feehan tossed the cigarette out the window and watched it smolder on the pavement like a dud firecracker. No wonder so many people were turning to pipes.

Working in a library had saved him from the habit of smoking. He did smoke at the *Messenger*. But then he wore a hat there, too, as Tuttle had in his office. It was on his typewriter at the *Messenger* that Jim Feehan had forged the Frank O'Rourke letters.

As a student of O'Rourke holographs, he had been struck by the similarity of type, and it had turned out that the machine was the very same model Frank had used. Not that the writer had confined himself to one typewriter, but the machine he had used for six years in San Bernardino was identical to the one Feehan had at the *Messenger.* The first time Feehan mimicked a Frank O'Rourke letter on the machine it had been a deliberate spoof. Except that Ninian had taken him seriously when he casually produced the letter.

"It isn't dated," Ninian observed.

"Frank often sent off letters without dating them."

"How long have you had it?"

Conscious of pressing against a limit, Feehan had said, "This one isn't ten years old."

"Do you have others?"

"I should say several dozen in all. We were quite close, Ninian."

Feehan had been a good deal more serious and considerably more careful when he typed up the other bogus Frank O'Rourke letters. He was not clear why he was doing this.

A first motive was the obvious one. The letters impressed people. They had certainly impressed Doris Hagstrom.

"How wise you were to keep them, Jim."

"I've kept all your letters too."

"I wish you hadn't." But she was clearly delighted.

It was one thing to fool people like Ninian and Doris; it would be quite another to deceive an expert. Jim Feehan had had no desire to succeed as a forger. What had started as a joke had gotten out of hand. But the real joke was that he did not fear the contempt of experts so much as the possibility Julian Moss would learn that Jim Feehan's famous O'Rourke letters were phonies. But even worse than that was imagining the reaction of Phyllis O'Rourke Mackin.

Phyllis had never liked Jim Feehan. She always made a point of telling people that Jim Feehan had not been her brother's friend. Alas, that was all too true. Even Phil Keegan had a better claim to have been Frank's friend than Feehan had.

The phone on the desk in his library office buzzed and Jim Feehan picked it up.

"There's a Paul Gardiner on the line."

"Tell him I'm not here."

Miss Potter made an embarrassed sound. "Mr. Feehan, I'm sorry, but I already told him you were in."

"Then tell him that I just stepped out of the office."

He banged down the phone. Miss Potter was cute as a button, but dumb. Worse, she was engaged, very much in love, and completely impervious to the Feehan charm. Indeed, she seemed unaware when he was exercising it. All the anger he felt for Gardiner was suddenly concentrated on his secretary. He had told her that he was not accepting calls from Paul Gardiner.

The door opened and Miss Potter peeked in, pretty as a picture. Her expression was not chastened.

"I told him you were indisposed."

"Good."

She closed the door behind her. The number Miss Potter had given him was 414–4514. Feehan thought of one of Frank's stories, a little tour de force called "He Dashed For Dot," in which an elementary code had figured, a correlation of the number series and the alphabet. He considered decoding, on that basis, the telephone number, but dismissed the idea as puerile. He picked up the phone and Miss Potter spoke in his ear.

"Please dial the number Paul Gardiner left."

"I gave it to you, Mr. Feehan."

He sighed. "Four-one-four, four-five-one-four."

After she started to dial, he decided he did not want her listening in. He told her he would complete the call and waited until she got off the line.

The phone rang once, twice. Then it was snapped up.

"Tuttle speaking."

"Tuttle!"

"Who's there?"

Jim Feehan replaced the phone, hanging up on his lawyer, a stunned expression on his face.

Gardiner's message did not need decoding after all.

9

THROUGH the scarcely opened Venetian blinds the swimming pool was visible in sections. The scene might have been a television picture that needed adjusting. By squinting his eyes, Roger Dowling could imagine a Christmas tree with the discontinuous green-blue glint of the water suggesting lights, tinsel, festivity. The darkened room in which they sat was not festive. There was the sound of ice cubes when Mrs. Mackin lowered her glass.

"Isn't it odd," she said. "Phil Keegan a friend of yours."

"Why?"

"A priest, a cop. But then I suppose priests are cops of a sort, aren't they?"

"In what way?"

"I gotcha! You know. The eye in the sky, somebody watching, you'll be sorry, all those rules."

"Is that what it seems like to you, religion?"

"It always did."

"Always? That's hard to believe. Did you attend parochial school when you were young?"

"Oh God, don't remind me. Sister Sarah Gertrude. We called her Sister Sour Grapefruit. Her weapon was a yardstick. Whammo. Right on the knuckles. Frank told me DIs in the Marine Corps were just like her."

"You mean your brother Frank?"

The little silence was irritated. Clearly she expected him to know that references to Frank were references to her brother.

"Yes, Frank's my brother. At least he was."

"Did he fall away too?"

Her laughter was hoarse and unmerry. She chuckled when she was done. "I haven't heard that phrase for years. Fallen away. Why not just left? Or freed himself?"

"And then he became famous?"

"Most of the fame has been posthumous. It's funny. While he was alive, he saw himself as a failure. So did I. He didn't exactly cover himself with glory during his last years. The novels, all three of them, were written within a space of five years, and early. Between the publication of his third novel and his death, ten years intervened. And he died young."

"How old?"

"Forty-four."

"How long ago was that?"

"Six years." She hadn't had to count.

"Was the money posthumous too?"

"What's that supposed to mean?"

"Didn't your brother leave you a lot of money?"

"If you don't mind my saying so, Father, that's a funny damned question."

"Your swimming pool suggests a general absence of money worries. As does this house."

"This house has seen a lot of worry."

"And your husband?"

"Has Phil Keegan told you about him?"

"He mentioned him. Why don't you tell me?"

"No. No, I don't think so. I see what you're trying to do, Father. You're not even subtle. I don't need your help. I'm all right. I've had troubles, everybody has troubles, but I'm doing fine."

"What are you drinking?"

"Do you want something?"

"No. I can't drink. I'm an alcoholic."

"Come on. A priest?"

"Oh, yes. I thought I was doing fine too, but I wasn't. My job . . ."

He told her about his job on the marriage court, told her about the anguish, about starting to drink and how it had gotten out of hand and brought him down.

"So they exiled you to Fox River?"

"I'm sure some people look at it that way. I did myself, at first. I don't anymore. Even though Saint Hilary's is not much of a parish."

"It was our parish. I wènt to grade school there."

"To Sister Sour Grapefruit?"

"Yeah. She might have been a saint, how would I have known, at that age? Imagine, spending your life facing seventh graders, year after year, no relief in sight. Do nuns ever retire? I suppose they must. I wonder if she's still alive."

"The school is a social center now. Even schools retire. Did your brother go there too?"

"Father, we were both baptized in that church and spent eight years in the parish school. We made our First Communion there, we were confirmed there. I was married at Saint Hilary's. So was Frank. Once. The first time. Is any of this news to you?"

"Yes, it is."

"I'm not within the parish boundaries, living here."

"We're less sticky about things like that than we used to be."

"At least you came to see *me*. Even though I don't much want you to. Most visitors want to talk about Frank. Dear God, what fantastic notions they have about him. The tragic hero, the romantic failure, the ironic vindication now that it's too late."

"That isn't how it was?"

"Of course not. You must know that. People's lives are far more alike than they're different. I still find it hard to believe that Frank is important to so many people, actually famous. But if that's fame, it doesn't amount to much. Frank would have agreed. Oh, he had an insatiable desire for praise, I suppose all writers do, but he was not someone to admire, he wasn't a hero. He was never a hero. Do you realize he had three wives?"

"That sounds heroic."

Her laugh was a surprised outburst of merriment. "I'm going to have another one of these," she said when she was done. "Sure you won't join me?"

"I would drink some coffee."

"A soft drink?"

"Fine."

He was standing at the window when she came back. He had tipped the blinds to a more open position.

"Do you ever use it?"

"The pool? Sometimes in the evening. I don't care for the sun."

"It seems a waste."

"It is. I didn't want it. Emil insisted. My husband. I think he had this vision of the two of us romping around out there, bronze, healthy, happy." Her voice fell away. "It's ironic, isn't it? It's Frank's money I live on now, not Emil's. Emil always wanted to be a good provider. And he was, while he was well. If there are any heroes, Emil's one, and look where he ended up." But the pity in her voice seemed directed at herself.

"And no one comes to ask you about Emil."

"No. It's always Frank. People don't seem to realize that I don't like being treated as if my only significance is in being the sister of Frank O'Rourke. Thank God he never lived in this house. They all want souvenirs. They'll steal anything if they can't buy it. His letters and papers fetch huge sums. There's a bookstore here in town that has a diary on display that Frank kept when he was a kid. You'd think it was a Gutenberg Bible."

"Have some things been published posthumously?"

"Oh sure. One collection of stories that Frank couldn't sell while he was alive. Some juvenilia. He was working on a novel when he died . . ."

"Will that be published?"

"It may be. People have suggested it. So far I've refused."

"Then you have it?"

"It's in my possession, yes." She spoke carefully, as if the point must be made with clarity.

"Why don't you want it published?"

"It's unfinished."

"Unfinished works of art have a special fascination."

"In this case, I'm sure Frank would agree."

"So you've read the book."

"I've read it. There isn't all that much. About a quarter of what he planned."

"Students of his work must be very anxious to see it."

"That's putting it mildly. I've been cajoled, threatened, pleaded with, practically implored. I've been offered sinful amounts of money. The fact that I say No only whets curiosity the more, but I don't see what I can do about that. The world doesn't really need an unfinished novel by Frank O'Rourke. So many of these people have a vested interest in Frank's reputation. There are so many parasitic professions."

"Most of us depend on others."

"You just don't quit, do you?"

"As a matter of fact, I do. I must be going. This has been very pleasant."

"Very pleasant? Maybe not as bad as you feared, but you don't have to kid me. I'm a recluse. It seems what I was destined to be. I like it."

A lonely woman in a darkened house, sipping on her wine from dawn to dusk. It seemed a pointless life, perhaps one of self-deception as well. If she thought little of her brother's work, why had she spent so much time telling him of it? There must be some association of priest, brother, and herself, the St. Hilary's of long ago.

That night, remembering Mrs. Mackin's remark that both she and her brother had been baptized at St. Hilary's, Roger Dowling went to the cabinet that contained the parish records. Frank O'Rourke had died at forty-four six years ago. The appropriate volume was not there. Roger Dowling searched the cabinet carefully. Nineteen forty-seven was not there. Frowning, he sat at his desk, filled his pipe deliberately, and, having lit it, sat puffing great pensive clouds of smoke about his head.

10

JIM FEEHAN entered Tuttle's office with a premonition of disaster. The receptionist with a cigarette in the corner of her mouth, the disreputable type lounging on the Naugahyde couch, seemed supporting players in a scenario heading for trouble.

"He's expecting ya," the girl said, her cigarette moving like a baton to the rhythm of her words.

And indeed Tuttle rose from behind his desk when Feehan entered. He wore no hat, his hair was slicked back, his expression was that of the man who has the bad news.

"What is it?" Feehan asked impatiently. Tuttle had been ridiculously guarded on the phone, and, rather than give Miss Potter cause for curiosity, Feehan had agreed to the lawyer's insistence that he come immediately.

"Sit down, Mr. Feehan."

"Tuttle, I don't have time to sit around. . . ."

Tuttle himself sat, bringing his outstretched down-turned palms floorward as he did so. Feehan sat down as if hypnotized.

"First of all, Mr. Feehan, I've been getting strange phone calls."

"Have you?"

"People call up and don't speak."

"Is that why you asked me here?"

"I wish it was. No, there is something else. Your letters."

Feehan crossed his legs and lit a cigarette, studying Tuttle as he did so. He had, he suddenly realized, put himself in this man's hands. Stupid Tuttle might be, but he was obviously cunning as well, which might be recompense enough. Would he have had suspicions about the authenticity of those letters?

"I want them back, Tuttle. Having them out of my hands makes me nervous. I don't care how secure your safe is. . . ."

Feehan stopped. Tuttle was scrubbing his face with his hands. Finally he peeked through his fingers at Feehan. "It is one of the best safes made, Mr. Feehan. I guarantee you that I will sue the manufacturer until . . ."

"Sue him! What the hell happened?"

What had happened was that Tuttle's office had been burglarized. The letters were missing.

"What else is missing?"

Tuttle's lips moved but no sound emerged. He pursed his lips, puffed his cheeks, closed his eyes. Then he spoke. "Nothing else is missing. Just the letters. They were after the letters, that's obvious. So you were right to worry."

Feehan leaped to his feet. "I've got to have those letters, Tuttle. I've got to!"

Feehan began to pace back and forth in the office, wild thoughts racing through his head. He was going to be disgraced, there was no doubt of it. Whoever had those letters would expose them as forgeries. He stopped in front of Tuttle's desk.

"Have you told the police?"

"Not formally."

"What the hell does that mean?"

Tuttle pressed a button on a box before him. An eerie voice emerged from it. It was like a seance.

"Delphine, send in Peanuts."

"I'm not hungry!" Feehan shouted.

Tuttle patted air, placating his client. The door opened and the man who had been lounging on the couch in the waiting room came in. After he had closed the door, carefully, he stood looking at Tuttle. He did not so much as glance at Feehan.

"This is Officer Pianone, Mr. Feehan. He is a member of the Fox River Police. Off duty, he is an associate of mine. He is now off duty."

"I don't want any publicity about those letters, Tuttle. On duty or off."

"Okay, okay. Then what we do is wait."

"Wait! What the hell for?"

"For the contact. What we don't know yet is do they appreciate the value of what they got. Unfortunately, the fact that they took only the letters and nothing but the letters strongly suggests they will ask a lot. Tell me, Mr. Feehan, how much would a lot amount to, as far as those valuable letters are concerned?"

"They're worthless."

Tuttle let his head roll sideways as a sad little smile twisted his lips. "Mr. Feehan, I know how you must feel. Think of how I feel. By God, I'll sue the company that makes that safe until they holler for mercy."

"No safe is safe," Officer Pianone opined.

"You may be right, Peanuts. But that isn't how they advertise the goddam thing." Tuttle turned to Feehan. "No, Mr. Feehan, forget the idea of trying to tell these people they got something worthless. They came for the letters, they took the letters."

"But how could they have known they were here?"

"Just why I wanted to talk to you. Exactly. What we have to do is go back over the last forty-eight hours. Whom might you have told about consulting me about those letters? Did you perhaps even suggest that they were now in a safe place and even where that safe place might be?"

"Of course I didn't. I talked to no one. No one even knew . . ." He stopped.

Tuttle sat forward. "Yes?"

But Feehan relaxed and shook his head. "No. No, they suggested I come see you but they don't know whether or not I took their advice."

"Names, please." Tuttle had picked up a pencil.

"Mervel of the *Messenger*. And Ninian."

Tuttle put the pencil down. He had not used it. "Reporters? Naw. Peanuts."

The heavyset man shifted his weight.

"Peanuts, what do you think? Does the MO suggest anyone?"

Feehan realized that the pained expression on the off-duty officer's face was the accompaniment of thought. Tuttle did not for long entertain the hope that the grimace was prelude to a helpful answer.

"Okay. No obvious suspects. We're back to what I said. We wait. We find out how much they want. After they make contact, we'll play it by ear. But I respect your request. No police."

Feehan glanced at Peanuts.

"Peanuts is off duty, Mr. Feehan. Right, Peanuts? See no evil, hear no evil?"

A bright smile took possession of Pianone's face.

"Are you related to the politicians?" Feehan asked.

Peanuts thought about that. Tuttle said that he was. He also suggested that Feehan keep close to his telephone.

"At your office. And at home. Who's at home?"

"No one. I'm not married."

"Lucky you. Chances are they'll know that. They'll call you where you are."

At that moment the telephone on Tuttle's desk rang and the three of them stared at it. In the silence they could hear the receptionist Delphine answer it. "Tuttle and Tuttle," she trilled on the other side of the closed door.

Feehan had asked about the other Tuttle. It stood for Tuttle's father. Tuttle Sr. had not been a lawyer, but he had helped his son through law school and was memorialized in the title of the firm. "More enduring than brass," Tuttle had said, when he told Feehan the story, digging a knuckle into the corner of his eye.

Now the box on Tuttle's desk buzzed. He picked up his phone.

"Who is it, Delphine?"

"He won't say."

"Did you tell him I was in?"

"I told him to hold."

Tuttle thought a minute. "Tell him I'm in conference. He can call back in five minutes."

Feehan waited through the five minutes with the others. They sat like three monkeys. See no evil, hear no evil, do no evil. It was during the wait it occurred to Feehan that one person who had certainly known about the letters was Tuttle himself. How convenient for the little lawyer that his client did not want the theft reported to the police. Feehan tried to remember if he had in any way conveyed to Tuttle that he would be reluctant to make a fuss if the letters were stolen. He was sure he had not. The whole tenor of their previous conversation had been the safety and security of the letters.

Five minutes went by and the phone did not ring. Ten minutes went by. Peanuts became fidgety. He left the office and when he came back he had a can of Coca-Cola that he drank as if with great thirst.

"That'll ruin your stomach," Tuttle said distractedly.

"So will hunger."

"You hungry?"

"It's nearly eleven."

Tuttle opened a drawer of his desk and took out a candy bar. Peanuts accepted it with a grin. The off-duty officer might have been a trained bear, or a very large and friendly dog. His relatives, the politicians, were reputed to be pillaging the city, but they were as innocent-looking as Peanuts and the voters apparently could not believe evil of them. Do no evil. Had Tuttle turned on his own client, staging a burglary? The phone call could be make-believe as well. Delphine had the look of an accomplice. Feehan got up from the chair into which he had slumped.

"Only you and I knew the letters were here, Tuttle. Did *you* happen to mention them to anyone?"

Tuttle's mouth dropped open in shocked surprise. "Mr. Feehan, you're my client. Our conversations are privileged. Anything you say to me . . ."

These protestations lost something from their practiced tone, as if Tuttle had had to make them often before.

"All I know, Tuttle, is that I mentioned them to no one."

"Maybe you was followed here," Peanuts said.

The theory brought Tuttle to his feet, as if in relief. He nodded his head vigorously in assent. "That's it!" His eyes narrowed shrewdly. "And if once, why not again? Peanuts, when Mr. Feehan leaves here, I want you to tail him. Understand? See if he is being followed. Keep an eye on him."

Feehan did not like it. He was the injured party and he was being treated as if he had led the thief to Tuttle's office. If only Tuttle and Peanuts were not so manifestly stupid, he could entertain the theory that they had conspired to rob him and then pretend that a third party was involved. In any case, he was glad he had not responded to Tuttle's query about the likely asking price for the letters.

But as he returned to his office in the library, it was not a blackmail demand that worried James Feehan. Now that the letters were in the open market, or at least in the black market, it was only a matter of time before they were discovered to be phonies. When that happpened, the prop would have been knocked from under Feehan's credibility. No one would ever again believe anything he said about Frank O'Rourke.

"Any calls, Miss Potter?"

"Not since you went away."

He looked at her. She was serious. Ye gods. But then he thought of Delphine and his pique went, giving way to the worry that should be occupying him.

Who in hell had those letters?

Sitting at his desk, he realized that he did not doubt for a moment who had them. He closed his eyes and the image of Paul Gardiner formed against his darkened lids.

11

WHEN Linda Moss took Paul Gardiner on the rounds of the Frank O'Rourke shrines, she felt like a kid. No, that wasn't it. She felt beautiful, desirable. Paul did that to her. The way he paid attention when she talked, the sense she had that, while he listened to her words, his ear was tuned to something deeper in her, something not spoken, the self that was her secret even from Julian.

Julian. She found herself wanting to apologize for her husband, to explain him, as if she were responding to some curiosity in Paul Gardiner about how she had actually ended up with such a drip. Drip. When had she last used that word?

"Did you grow up in Fox River?"

"Oh yes." She made it sound like a concession to incredulity. "I've been here forever. All my life."

"It's a nice town."

"Where are you from?"

His eyes, narrowed against the sun, seemed to be scanning far horizons. "Out west. California."

She laughed. "I never think of California as west."

"You'd have a helluva time finding it going east. But I know what you mean. Now what's this?"

"Well, it used to be a school. A Catholic school. It's where Frank O'Rourke went to grade school. Eight years in all, right here. I don't know what it's used for now. Some parish thing or other." In the playground elderly people were playing shuffleboard or sitting under umbrellas, playing cards. "And that's the church. You know he was a Catholic?"

Paul Gardiner nodded.

She said, "Are you?"

"I'm not anything."

"Neither are we. Oh, Julian is, in a way," she amended. Suddenly she did not want to share with her husband the distinction of inhabiting agnostic wastelands with Paul Gardiner. It made her feel lonely and a little bit of a heroine to be existing in a universe without God. Until Paul asked her, she had not known she doubted God's existence. "Do you want to look at the school?"

"No."

"I don't know if we can go into the church."

"That's all right. What else is there?"

"Have you seen Jim Feehan, by the way?"

His cool eyes turned to her. "Feehan?"

"The one who has O'Rourke letters. He was some sort of boyhood friend of O'Rourke's, although Julian is skeptical about that. What's for sure is that he knows O'Rourke's work like nobody else."

"What's the sister like?"

Linda was prepared to bubble forth the hearsay she

had gathered over the years, but she didn't. With Paul Gardiner she was determined to be as honest as she could be.

"I've never met her. I saw her once, but I've never met her. She won't discuss her brother with anyone."

"Why not?"

Linda shrugged. "I only know what I hear. Apparently she isn't as enthralled by his memory as some others are."

"Like you and Julian?"

"Oh, I'm not all that uncritical an admirer myself. I mean of him as a person. The way he treated his wives and children!"

"You said you saw the sister once. When was that?"

Linda smiled sheepishly. "I just went and hung around her house until I saw her. I saw the husband too. He's in a wheelchair."

"She must see someone."

"I'm sure she has friends and all that. What she won't respond to are requests to talk about her brother Frank. She just refers people to her lawyer."

"What could he tell them?"

"Bill Florey? Not much. He takes care of her."

Apparently the implication had gotten into her tone. Perhaps she had meant it to. In any case, Paul Gardiner picked it up.

"How do you mean, takes care of her?"

"Well, you know. The business side of her brother's estate."

"And that's all?" His smile was encouraging.

"There's gossip. Say, why don't we drive past her house? It's quite a place. Who knows, we may get a glimpse of her."

She said it with a lilt in her voice, a proposal of adventure, of fun. And he said, "Why not?" and off they went. As they cruised along the river drive, slowly, past the great houses that stood far back from the street on well-cared-for lawns liberally dotted with trees and shrubbery, Linda let the neighborhood speak for itself. When they came to the Mackin house, she went even more slowly, her foot entirely off the pedal, and for once she didn't care that Julian insisted on having the idling speed set so high. It was more than enough to keep them moving along at five miles an hour.

"They'll think we're casing the joint," she said.

"Yeah." He said it out of the corner of his mouth. Laughing, she reached out to slap his arm. To her surprise, he caught her hand. Still holding it, he turned toward the house.

"The house that Frank O'Rourke built," he murmured.

"Oh, he never lived there."

"I meant his money."

"I suppose."

"What does her husband do?"

"Well, nothing now. I told you, he's in a wheelchair. But you're right about her brother's money. She's rich now and they weren't rich before. Should I stop?"

He shook his head. "The property looks out over the river?"

"That's right."

"What's on the other side?"

Rather than try to describe it for him, she drove to the Stratton Bridge, crossed, and came up the west river road from the marina to a point that looked across the Fox River toward the Mackin house. It was a picnic area with playing fields, outdoor grills, and, on the bluff overlooking the river, a parking place. A parking place frequented in the dark by lovers.

"Mulholland Drive," Paul said.

"What's that?"

"A place like this. A place to neck."

Again he took her hand and for a moment she had a choice. She could regard it as a little joke, something unserious that could be laughed away, whether or not she withdrew her hand immediately. Or she could do what she did: turn her body toward him, look him solemnly in the eye, and wait for him to make the next move.

He made it. He took her firmly but gently in his arms and kissed her long and passionately on the lips. Then he held her tightly against him, looked out across the river, and said, "To a stranger, they all look alike. The houses over there."

She found herself pointing out which house was the Mackins', her heart thundering within her. She was being unfaithful to Julian, or the next thing to it, and she was not a damned bit sorry. She was excited. She could sit here forever with Paul Gardiner and she was especially glad it was here, as if this parking lot with all its memories and associations with youth redeemed the dull years she had spent as Mrs. Julian Moss.

"Well," she said, "that's about it. You've seen it all."

For answer, he kissed her, and she strained against him. Was he married? She didn't know and she didn't care. She half hoped he was, as if that might balance out any unfairness to Julian that was involved.

"Not quite all."

"Oh?"

"The diary."

"But you've already seen . . ."

He was smiling. She smiled. She understood. Back to the bookstore. Back to where she lived. Necking by the river was fine for kids, but they were no longer kids. Linda surprised herself with the matter-of-fact way she nodded, started the car, and backed out of their parking space.

They went instead to his motel, The Redbird, an establishment whose years of prosperity had been cut short when the Interstate was routed half a mile to the south. Now it relied on the weary motorist who was willing to drive this far from the Interstate in search of lodgings, and on furtive couples. Like us, Linda thought. She felt uneasy getting out of the car, and while she waited for Paul to unlock the door of his unit she half expected the manager to plunge out of his office, shouting that he had rented the unit to Paul alone, not to a couple.

"Why on earth did you choose this place?" she asked, when he pushed the door open.

"One motel is like another. I'll turn on the air conditioning."

He did not turn on the lights and she was grateful to him for that, though there was something eerie about taking off her clothes in the semidark of the motel room with the air conditioner wheezing and rattling in the window. Paul was there only in silhouette. She heard him pull back the covers on the bed and then his hand took hers and tugged her into adultery.

Afterward, he insisted that he wanted to see the diary again. She talked incessantly as they drove to Reading Matters and kept her eye on the road. She had avoided looking directly at Paul once they had risen from the bed and turned on the light. She did not want to think of what they had done. She wanted her mind to be a blank slate. Paul Gardiner wanted to see the diary? Fine. They would go to the bookstore. What then? She did not know. She did not want to think of the future any more than she wanted to think of the past. Forming within her, like an imaginary baby, moving swiftly through the stages of gestation, were the promise of hysteria, the threat of tears, the onslaught of an overwhelming sense of remorse.

They had not been in the store five minutes when a car door slammed outside. It was Paul who hurried to the window.

When he turned toward her, there was a look of alarm on his face.

"It's a priest."

"A priest!"

"I don't want to be here when he comes in." He tried to smile. "Priests make me jumpy. Where can I hide?"

She pointed to the door leading to their living quarters. He dashed for it and it closed behind him just as the street door opened and the priest came in. He stepped to one side and looked at the jangling bell over the door with a little smile on his lean face.

"It reminds me of a sacristy bell."

"I don't understand."

"When a priest comes out to say Mass . . . It doesn't matter. I'm a priest."

"I can see that."

"And I can see that I make you uncomfortable. Don't be." He looked around. "What a lovely bookstore. I've heard about it, of course. I'm sorry I haven't come before."

She was conscious of Paul Gardiner in the apartment and she didn't like the thought of his being in there, alone, with all their private things. That was a thought she had to expunge, particularly with this priest standing right here. He had appeared out of nowhere like the wrath of God, although there was certainly nothing wrathful about him. Linda was suddenly fearful that she would burst into tears. No wonder Catholics go to confession. She wanted desperately to tell someone she had done something very wrong and now she was sorry and this priest looked like a man who could hear awful things without surprise or condemnation. She wanted to tell God that she was sorry.

"My name is Roger Dowling. I'm the pastor of Saint Hilary's parish. I've got all the books of Frank O'Rourke, but I wondered what you might have *about* him. Nothing too academic, you understand. Has there been a biography written?"

"No, I don't think so. There are cassettes."

"Tapes?"

"Yes. He did some interviews for a California radio station, and they're available on cassettes. Do you have a machine?"

He nodded. "As a matter of fact, I do. I bought it to play C. S. Lewis tapes on."

Linda showed him the cassettes. There were three different interviews and he wanted only one, so they had to talk about which tape it should be. Linda wanted desperately for him to leave the store. She wanted to get Paul Gardiner out of their apartment.

"Why don't you just take all three and listen to them at home? Bring back the ones you don't want."

"But that wouldn't be fair. You'd end up with second-hand tapes. Look, I'll take . . ." He closed his eyes and pointed. "That one. How much is it?"

After he had paid, his eye went briefly to the corner of erotica, and again Linda felt a mad urge to cry out what she had done and rid herself of guilt.

"Did you say Saint Hilary's? Isn't that where . . ."

"Where Frank O'Rourke went to school? Yes."

When he was gone, she locked the door and ran back to the apartment. She burst in, calling Paul's name.

There was no answer.

She knew immediately that the apartment was empty. He had gone. By the back door. Of course. But why? She should have felt relief but, irrationally, she was angry, as if she had wanted to rush into his arms, perhaps repeat the act of love here in the apartment.

She wandered through the small rooms, still keeping

the past and future at bay. It was now, only now, an unrelated moment. She had not been unfaithful to her husband.

And then she noticed that the glass case that had contained the diary of Frank O'Rourke was gone.

12

DORIS Hagstrom and Agnes Florey walked briskly up the driveway toward the front entrance of the Mackin residence. The
two women wore tailored suits, medium high heels, and their
hair was done with uncharacteristic exuberance. Most uncharacteristic of all was the amount of make-up each was
wearing.

"The place looks deserted," Agnes said.

"Doesn't it, though."

Doris had once practiced trying to speak while holding
a full smile, the way the girls in the television commercials do. It
had reminded her of unsuccessful efforts to learn ventriloquism
when she was a child. She did no better now, trying to speak to
Agnes while retaining a bright empty-headed expression for
anyone who might be watching their approach.

As they neared the house, a problem presented itself.

Where, precisely, was the main door? The driveway bifurcated at the pool, one part going off toward the garage, the other sweeping past the house, but where it passed the house there was only a wall of glass.

"The French doors?" Agnes suggested.

"I wish you had asked Bill."

"Bill! If he knew I was here he'd kill me."

The two women stopped on the driveway between pool and house and looked around, still smiling brightly. But doubt and indecision had crept into their eyes. At a whirring sound they turned. The French doors opened and, emerging from them, was a man in a wheelchair. His head swung loosely on his shoulders and he seemed unable to steady it and look at them.

"Good afternoon," Doris said brightly.

"Avon calling," Agnes chirped.

The man in the wheelchair circled them once, then went off toward the pool. Doris, emitting a little cry, started after him, certain the invalid would end up in the water. But before she reached the chair and before the chair reached the pool, the man veered to the right and seemed to accelerate as he crossed the patio.

"It's all right," someone called. "Don't worry about him."

A middle-aged man in workclothes had come around a corner of the house. He was bearded and carried huge trimming shears in his gloved hand. The bridge of his glasses had been repaired with adhesive tape.

"Anything I can do for you ladies?"

"Do you work here?" Doris asked frostily.

"Work and live here. I take care of the yard, the house, minor repairs, that sort of thing. What do you ladies do?"

"We have come to see the lady of the house," Doris said, turning away.

Agnes put a hand on her friend's arm. "Doris, wait."

A new plan had flicked through her mind and she only hoped Doris would fall in with it quickly.

"Actually, you may be the one we want to see," Agnes said to the man. "We're from the county agent."

"I thought I heard you mention Avon."

Agnes's laughter was a girlish trilling. "Did you hear that? A little joke. Do we look like cosmetic salespersons?"

The man nodded. "Yes, you do."

"We'll take that as a compliment." Agnes turned brisk. "How many Chinese elms on this property?"

"How many?"

"Surely there are some."

"Of course there are. We've had several taken down already. Maybe eight or nine."

"Left or taken down?"

"I haven't counted the ones remaining."

"Let's do it then. Let's start right here." Agnes pointed across the pool to where a trellised arch led to a large expanse of lawn liberally covered with trees.

The bearded yardman squinted at her through his cloudy glasses and his mustache twitched in thought. "All right," he said finally. "Let's go count elms."

He set out ahead of them and Agnes looked at Doris. She raised her eyes and pantomimed relief. Doris rounded her eyes as if to ask Why?

But it had seemed to Agnes that an interview with the yardman was as good a start as any on the literary project she and Doris were embarked upon.

She became convinced of this when they had gone into the further yard and were seated on a bench, bracketing the yardman. Agnes had switched on the miniature recorder she had taken from Bill's den, as soon as they sat down.

"I'm Agnes and this is Doris," she began. "What's your name?"

"Call me Ishmael."

"My, aren't you a cultivated yardman, though." Agnes poked him in the ribs with an index finger. "Why not Ahab?"

The man grinned. "My name is Herman."

"Melville?"

"I'm serious. Call me Hermie. Everyone does."

"Everyone? Even Mrs. Mackin?"

He nodded and pointed out across the lawn. "There are three elms there, overlooking the river."

"How long have you worked here?"

"What difference does that make?"

"Just curious."

"Five years, maybe a little more."

"You must like it here."

"Well, look around. It's nice property. It's secluded. I'm left pretty much to myself. Usually."

"Mrs. Mackin sounds like a pretty good boss."

Hermie studied her for half a minute. "What exactly are you two after, anyway?"

"Have you ever heard of Frank O'Rourke?"

"What about him?"

"He was a famous writer. He grew up here in Fox River. Mrs. Mackin is his sister. You must have known that."

"What if I did?"

"Hermie, you're right. We're not here to count elms. The two of us, Doris and I, are writing a book about Frank O'Rourke. From the local angle, the Fox River angle. That means we want to write about his sister."

"Then you'd better talk to her."

"Wait. We hope to. But when you came up, it occurred

to me that it would be a good idea to get a sense of the atmosphere around here first. From you."

"The little man's view?"

"Well, the view of someone who works here, who keeps the place looking so nice. And it is nice, it looks fabulous. Hermie, you could be in the book. By name. What do you think of that?"

"Are you two from Fox River?"

"Yes. Both of us." Agnes leaned toward him. "My husband is Mrs. Mackin's lawyer."

"You're Mrs. Florey?"

"Do you know my husband?"

"Well, I know who Mr. Florey is." Hermie combed his beard with the fingers of one hand, looking at Agnes out of the corner of his eye. "Why don't you ask your husband to bring you along when he comes to talk to Mrs. Mackin?"

"He won't."

"He won't?"

"He says she absolutely refuses to talk to people. Isn't that true? That's why we got all dressed up like this."

He snorted and shook his head. "What kind of book do you plan to write?"

Doris said, "Descriptions of places associated with Frank O'Rourke."

"Opinions about him from people who knew him," Agnes added.

Doris said, "You didn't by any chance know him, did you?"

"Know him? Lady, this is all news to me."

"You've been here more than five years and you didn't know your boss is the sister of a famous writer?"

"Why in hell would I know a thing like that?"

"He's right," Agnes said.

"Then what's the point of talking to him?"

"That's a good question," Hermie agreed.

"I'll tell you why. I want a description of what life is like here. A typical day. What's she like? What's she like to her husband, how does she treat him? That was her husband in the wheelchair, wasn't it?"

"Yes, it was. A typical day? Okay, I'll give you a typical day."

He leaned back on the bench, took off his glasses, and stared out over the river and began to talk. The two women listened, impatient at first, then interested, finally unaware that the man was holding them spellbound. He spoke of the seasons and their alteration, he spoke of the phases of the moon, he spoke of the difference between the morning hours in November and in May. When he paused to light a pipe, Agnes spoke.

"You haven't mentioned the Mackins."

"I don't see much of the Mackins. I'll tell you something. I dream this is really my place. I'm not working for them, I'm working for me. They don't give a damn about the property. He can't and she's always in the house. So I imagine this place is mine."

"You say you live here?"

"Over the garage."

The whirring sound of the wheelchair warned them of the approach of Mr. Mackin. He came bouncing over the lawn, his head swinging freely, eyes rolling, emitting a kind of mewling sound.

"The poor man," Doris said.

"Won't he go over the cliff?"

Hermie shook his head and sure enough the wheelchair made a great arcing turn and Mr. Mackin headed back toward the house.

"How sad," Agnes said.

"Sad? I don't know. Sometimes I think he's the happiest person I know. You heard him singing."

"Singing?"

"That's what he was doing."

"You could have fooled me," Agnes said.

13

LINDA Moss had been wrong to suggest that there had been no biography written of Frank O'Rourke, although her error was mitigated by the fact that most of the books ostensibly devoted to his life were chiefly concerned with detailed analyses of O'Rourke's creative works. Father Dowling found the bare facts he wanted by consulting the relevant volume of *Contemporary American Authors* and an old volume of *Who's Who*.

"You don't need me," Phil Keegan complained. "What you want is a gossip columnist, someone like that."

"I thought you could send a wire to California."

"To where in California?"

"Well, by and large, he lived in San Bernardino."

"Look, Roger, first check with Flo Eberle at the *Messenger*. If she can't help you, I'll see what I can do. Just tell me one thing. What the hell difference does it make now what happened to the wives of Frank O'Rourke?"

"I don't know."

When Roger Dowling entered the *Messenger* building, people looked at him the way people often look at a priest, as a harbinger of disaster, perhaps come to anoint a stricken soul or on some similarly somber mission. At the information counter, the girl looked up and, at the sight of his clerical garb, turned suddenly and comically serious.

"Yes, what is it?"

"I'd like to see Flo Eberle, please."

"Flo Eberle? Are you sure?"

"I didn't make an appointment, but I would be very grateful if I could have a few minutes of her time."

"Flo Eberle, our entertainment editor?"

"Is that her title?"

"Yes. She writes movie reviews and she comments on TV programs, that sort of thing. Is she the one you want to see?"

"If she isn't busy, yes."

The girl's name was engraved in white letters on the black plastic badge pinned to her blouse. Jane Sisson. She sighed and picked up the phone, her expression suggesting she had done all that could be expected of her. When her call went through, she stared steadily to the right of Roger Dowling.

"Miz Eberle? There is a priest here to see you." Pause. "Yes, a priest. I'll ask." Her eyes moved to the left and she smiled. "I forgot to ask your name."

"Roger Dowling."

"Reverend Roger Dowling?"

"Father Dowling will do."

The girl took her hand from the receiver. "His name is Father Dowling, Miz Eberle. He wants a few minutes of your time."

Whatever was being said in the girl's ear, it was clearly nothing she wanted Father Dowling to overhear. She pressed the receiver tightly against her hair and her eyes darted from object to object. When she took the phone away from her ear, Father Dowling had the impression that Flo Eberle had already hung up.

"I guess you can go up."

"Guess?"

"She thinks it's a joke." The girl tried to smile. "Lately people have been playing practical jokes on her. She was called back from lunch to take a long-distance call from Rock Hudson. A telegrammed invitation to take part in an interview with Jane Fonda was a hoax. She's in no mood. I'm quoting."

"Where is her office?"

He took the elevator to the third floor and went down a long corridor past open doors. In each office, there was a desk and someone looking out as he went by. Flo Eberle was at the end of the corridor, on the left. Her door was closed. When he knocked she shouted her question.

"What is it? I'm busy."

He turned the knob but the door would not open.

"I said I'm busy. Who is it?"

"Roger Dowling."

Silence.

He looked back down the corridor. Heads had emerged from the open doors and he noticed that some faces wore expectant conspiratorial smiles. A lock turned in Flo Eberle's door. It opened slowly, a crack.

"My God!"

"Flo Eberle?"

"Are you really a priest?"

"For over a quarter of a century."

The door opened wide and a small woman with an enormous hairdo and eyes that bulged looked up at him.

"I thought they were kidding. Downstairs, I mean. You wouldn't believe the nuts in this place. Come in, come in."

Along one wall a row of television sets, their audio inaudible, beamed different pictures into the room. As Father Dowling looked, each screen dimmed and immediately commercial messages came on. Were the networks really synchronized? Roger Dowling's eye had been drawn to the sets by Flo Eberle's darting gaze.

"I gotta watch them."

"I see." In the line of duty?

She punched a button on a remote-control panel on her desk and one of the sets began to talk. A woman with hair in her eyes was speaking throatily of a movie currently being made in Hollywood.

"She means Streisand," Flo said after a moment, addressing some unseen audience. Her readers? She punched the button and the set went quiet again.

"Captain Keegan suggested I come to you with the questions I have."

"The police?" Her look was wary again. "What did you say your name is?"

"Roger Dowling."

"And the cop who sent you is Keegan?"

"That's right."

She circled her desk, picked up the phone, and asked for police headquarters. She stood looking at Father Dowling as she waited.

"Captain Keegan, please. Captain Keegan? Flo Eberle of the *Messenger*. One question. Did you send a priest named Dowling over here? Okay. No, no reason. I just wanted to make sure. No, it's all right. He's here now. Thank you, Captain. Good-by."

She sat down and waved a limp hand at a chair for Roger Dowling.

"Sorry about that, but this place has become a squirrel cage. What can I do for you?"

"You know the name Frank O'Rourke?"

"Of course."

"Do you know he was married several times?"

She sat forward, elbows on her desk. "Three times, to be exact. One wife dead, two still living."

She was the right one to come to, there was no doubt of that. With minimal checking she produced the wedding dates and maiden names of O'Rourke's three wives.

On January 3, 1947, Francis Anthony O'Rourke had married Lorraine Dolan in the church of St. Hilary, Fox River, Illinois. She died. On April 1, 1964, in Reno, Nevada, he had married Gretchen van den Dingler. Flo looked over the half glasses she had put on to read. "That's Greta Vanden, of course. A terrible actress but built like a brick chateau. Finally, just seven years ago, he married a practical nurse he met in a sanatarium. He was living with her, and off her, while he worked on his final novel."

"I don't suppose you would have anything on Lorraine Dolan?"

"She's dead. I told you that."

"But she and O'Rourke had children?"

"Two boys."

"Where are they?"

Flo looked wide-eyed across the desk, thinking. Her eyes went from time to time to the bank of television sets that kept her apprised of the daytime fare of the three television networks. And then she had it.

"They went with Greta as part of the divorce settlement. Weird but true. His sons to the custody of their stepmother. Of course she married again."

Roger Dowling considered those two boys moved like pawns through a complicated game created by the unruly loins and appetites of their elders. What on earth had happened to them? Flo's curiosity, too, was piqued.

"It would make a story, wouldn't it? Lost sons of famous novelist."

"But why forgotten? I should have thought they would have been sought out by all these people who are so interested in the father's work. They are very avid people, these scholars."

"I'll find out," Flo decided. "I'll make some calls. I'll find out."

"Would you let me know when you do?"

"You have aroused my professional interest, Father Dowling. If there is a story here, I mean to write it."

"All I want to know is what happened to those boys."

"Why is it important to you?"

"Their parents were married in my church."

The explanation was baffling enough to be accepted by Flo Eberle. She promised Roger Dowling she would let him know what she learned of the sons of Frank O'Rourke even before she wrote her story.

"If anything comes of it, I owe you that, at least."

14

THE PRICE Paul Gardiner asked for the return of Feehan's phony letters was the unfinished novel Frank O'Rourke had been writing at the time of his death.

"But I don't have it. You know I don't have it. It is in the possession of his sister."

Paul Gardiner's gray eyes became colder still. "That's the price, Feehan."

"How in hell can I give you what I don't have?"

"Get it."

"I couldn't afford it and anyway it's not for sale."

"Get it."

It emerged that Paul Gardiner was suggesting he become a thief. Suggesting, hell. This was blackmail.

They sat in Feehan's office at the branch library. Miss Potter, schooled by Feehan's dissatisfaction with her telephone manner, had stepped into his office rather than announce his visitor.

"It's the one who phoned."

"The one who phoned," he repeated sarcastically.

"You know. He left a number."

"Describe him."

Miss Potter's face brightened. "Oh, he's very good-looking. Tall."

"Did you ask his name?"

The glow left her face. She had done it again. It was a mystery to her why he didn't fire her, she had admitted as much, and if it was not a mystery to Jim Feehan, neither was it rational. Oh, granted firing anyone in these litigious times is to court a lawsuit, perhaps even provoke a platoon of young government lawyers representing the underdog as redefined by some legislative novelty, but that was not it. Miss Potter was not the suing kind. But if he was the pursuing kind, she refused to be his quarry. Indeed, she acted as if she were unaware of his overtures. She baffled him. That she was in love and engaged was as it should be, but surely there must be warm blood inside those alabaster limbs and some taint of the race's corruption in her girlish heart.

"His name is Paul Gardiner," Feehan informed her.

"Then you know him." She seemed to think this exonerated her. "Should I show him in?"

Feehan felt ready for the thief. He had rehearsed this encounter dozens of times since his unsatisfactory session with Tuttle and the ineffable Peanuts. As between his own tapping out of a few allegedly O'Rourkian letters and Gardiner's breaking into Tuttle's safe, there was simply no comparison. The latter was an undoubted crime, the former a peccadillo at most. After all, had he defrauded anyone? Had he made so much as a red cent from those letters? He had never even shown them to anyone who mattered, anyone who might have been misled by their contents into publishing some palpable nonsense about Frank O'Rourke. No, he had used the letters for gentler and more private purposes. They had provided entree to more than one susceptible female heart, willing to settle for glamour at one remove, a carnal exchange with a man who had known the man who had written. . . . Jim Feehan sometimes felt like a second-class relic. Agnes Florey had been the most recent to succumb to the blandishments of those letters. Indeed, Feehan had written yet another with an eye to Agnes's peculiar predilections, a letter in which Frank O'Rourke had gone on about his dear friend Jim Feehan's ability to plumb the depths of the female heart, thanking him for the insights that had enabled the novelist to give new dimensions to the character of Clara in "Special Dispensation."

"Oh, I love that story," Agnes had said.

"You're very much like her, you know. Clara." Feehan leaned forward and added a dollop of brandy to their glasses. He put Agnes's glass in her hands. She looked up at him, not Agnes Florey now, but the Clara Owens of Frank O'Rourke's story. Dear God, the power of imaginative literature. Including, of course, his forged letters.

That had been the innocent extent of his exploitation of his manufactured memorabilia. Of course he had allowed it to be bruited about that he had this invaluable cache of O'Rourke letters and he had written more replies than he cared to remember diverting academic bloodhounds from his trail. He had invented—why not?—a pledge he had made to Frank during the author's last weeks. Jim Feehan would have no part in any posthumous exploitation of his friend's work and fame. When researchers were importunate enough to telephone, it was possible to put a cutting edge to his voice as he recalled his imaginary vow, thus suggesting that his caller was a cynical necromancer unworthy of his valuable time.

Paul Gardiner, he had assumed, was merely the latest Frank O'Rourke fan to make the mandatory pilgrimage to Fox River. Of course he would hear, if he had not already heard, of the letters cherished by Jim Feehan. Feehan had anticipated no difficulty at all in deflecting the young man to other, and more genuine, objects of interest.

But Paul Gardiner was a more serious collector than he had imagined. He would have to take a stern and lofty tone with the young man.

He said, "Mr. Gardiner, I am afraid you are going to have to be content with those letters. At least for the nonce. Surely you don't imagine you can steal with impunity."

"Steal? I'm afraid it was your lawyer who stole the letters. From you, that is. He tried to sell them to me."

"Tuttle did that?"

"The point is that the letters are fake. Anyone who spent ten minutes with them would recognize them as fakes."

Feehan considered contesting the accusation, then thought better of it. Of course Gardiner was right. Only an Agnes Florey, under the influence of soft lights, strong brandy, and subtle flattery, could be impressed by those letters. And Ninian and Mervel, of course, but what the hell did that prove?

"So you want me to steal Frank's unfinished novel from his sister?"

"That's right." Paul Gardiner stood. "You have forty-eight hours."

"That long? Where can I get in touch with you?"

Gardiner smiled grimly. "Feehan, I am not a fool. I will contact you two days from now. You give me the manuscript, I return your letters."

Perhaps it was the prospect of forty-eight hours' reprieve that led him to agree almost insouciantly to this outrageous proposal. In two days anything could happen. He would think of something.

He thought of nothing that afternoon. He told Miss Potter "No calls" and sat in his office with the lights out, sipping sherry and staring at the window where a dull day seemed a visible symbol of his flaccid brain. He could not think. He was not exactly worried. . . . A man like Jim Feehan does not get turned into a thief by fiat, no matter the cards Paul Gardiner held. No one knew better than Jim Feehan that it was his vanity that conferred strength on Gardiner's threat. He repeated the simple truths of the situation. He had defrauded no one. He had not published any forged letter as genuine. He had gained nothing of a tangible, economically tangible, sort from the really rather innocent game he had played. Morally he had exploited his dead friend. Not friend, acquaintance. The gray day at the window seemed to invite equally gray truths. He had not been an intimate friend of Frank O'Rourke. He realized it had been a very long time since he had admitted this, even to himself. A sad smile formed on his lips. That was why he was so good a persuader. He persuaded himself first of all. By the time he sat in the soft light with a woman like Agnes Florey, he was himself completely convinced of the truth of his lies. Frank and I. I remember . . . One time, I'll never forget it . . . And all the while keeping his eyes on the point of these fictive memories, using Frank as he did the brandy and the soft lighting, as an instrument of seduction. He might learn to be ashamed of that, but it was not an indictable offense. Adultery. His smile became cynical. Get all you can. That was an axiom he shared with Frank O'Rourke, no doubt about it. But his practiced method presupposed a literate woman, or at least one suggestibly romantic. Miss Potter, like many who work in libraries, never read, and if there was a romantic bone in her body, Jim Feehan had yet to locate it.

Tuttle. What ignominy to be done in by someone as

small bore as the lawyer. Feehan could believe now that Ninian and Mervel had put him onto Tuttle in a deliberate attempt to make a fool of him. They must never know the extent of their success. Oddly, he felt little anger toward Tuttle. If there was an object of his anger, it was himself.

He got drunk. Almost to his surprise, he emptied the decanter of sherry he kept in a cabinet beneath the window in his office. He went to the closet where he kept a case. He had meant merely to decant another bottle, but he refilled his glass as well. When Miss Potter buzzed to say she was leaving, he had to speak very carefully, as if his tongue were wearing a glove.

Agnes was surprised when he phoned her and he did not even try to disguise the fact that he had been drinking. She told him he sounded drunk.

"And lonely."

"Jim, for heaven's sake. It's seven-thirty in the evening. Where are you?"

"My office. Come to the library. Check something out."

"You're drunk," she repeated, but there was a thoughtful overtone in her voice. He heard the little catch of excitement. Their affair represented her first real departure from a lifetime of rectitude. But he had rightly guessed that her humdrum life had not stifled her romantic imagination. His guess had been based on what Doris had told him. Had the one woman talked to the other about him? That was the only way either would learn of the special link he had become between them. He never talked.

"Haven't you got an overdue book or something?"

"Stay there," she said, after another pause.

He hung up. Well, at least he had given her a good excuse for going out. "I'm going to the library." What husband could object to that?

15

Jɪᴍ'ꜱ ᴄᴀʟʟ could not have come at a worse time, or at a better, depending on how Agnes Florey chose to look on it.

This had been the worst day of her life. Doris, when she told Agnes, had cried as hard as she did. The two friends stood in the Florey kitchen, clinging to each other and weeping as if the world had come to an end. And, indeed, in some sense, it had for Agnes Florey.

Her tears expressed many things: shock, anger, the sense of being wounded so deeply she could never possibly heal. But tears also postponed the need to talk about it. Sincere as she was sure Doris's tears were, the thought of discussing *this* with her best friend, even if she had learned of it through her best friend, had something of the unthinkable about it. Doris would not have been her best friend if she had not told Agnes. Agnes had no difficulty with that. If their roles had been reversed, she would have told Doris. And, no point in trying to deceive herself, no matter how hard she would have tried not to, she would have felt a perverse pleasure in being the bearer of such deliciously awful news.

"She's years older than Bill," Doris sobbed. "It doesn't make any sense. It doesn't make any sense at all."

"How did you find out?"

Doris stepped back and blinked her tear-filled eyes. "Agnes, did you already know?"

Agnes shook her head violently. "No!" She had not even remotely suspected Bill of infidelity.

Infidelity. What other word was there for it? It was the only word she knew. It was the word she had used to describe her own affair with Jim Feehan. Affair. Another archaic word. Agnes felt linguistically out of date, but her vocabulary matched her outlook. It was a moral outlook, one that had never really been seriously disturbed by the steamy fiction that was her steady diet.

"I think of it as research," she had told Bill, when he commented on the nature of the novels she brought home from the library by the armful. "I'm studying the market."

Find out what the public wants, that was the idea. It turned out she herself was part of the public who wanted this sort of novel. Yet when she daydreamed of being a writer and of publishing a novel, it was always something vaguely early nineteenth century. *Pride and Prejudice. Jane Eyre. The Old Curiosity Shop.* This suggested that her real self existed at a definitive moral distance from the outlook of the popular novels she devoured. And then Jim Feehan had come along and she discovered she was as unreasoning and self-destructive as any of the heroines whose exploits she followed so avidly.

Frank O'Rourke. Her life seemed to swing around this dead author: the book with Doris, talking about him with his old friend Jim Feehan, and then finding out that the librarian and book-page editor had had a surprising hand in the construction of some of O'Rourke's most famous stories. His recognition of a similarity between her and Clara Owens had seemed to Agnes a revelation of unsuspected depths of her being. Clara. Of course. And Frank O'Rourke had written in a letter that he had depended on Jim Feehan's remarks in the creation of the character.

"Who was Clara?" she had asked Jim in a whisper, wanting and not wanting to know the real counterpart of her fictional self.

"You."

She squeezed his hand. "No, I mean the girl you had in mind when you told Frank . . ."

"You. I mean it. I think I imagined you even then, long before I knew you. Even now, you don't seem wholly substantial to me, completely real."

It was wonderful. Did she love Jim Feehan? In some sense of the term, of course she did, but she loved the adventure far more. It was real and unreal. The whole thing might have been happening in a book rather than in Jim's apartment. That was why it had been so difficult for her to feel remorse and not even the use of terms like "affair" and "infidelity" had helped.

How then could she feel so utterly betrayed when Doris came to tell her that Bill was having an affair with Phyllis O'Rourke Mackin? Yet she had known immediately it was true.

"Agnes, you weren't skeptical or doubtful, not even for a minute."

"I know. It's as if I had known all along."

"But you didn't?"

"No." And then dreamily she added, "Not consciously."

Doris nodded in deference to this suggestion of an intuitive gift. But what Agnes felt was the moral fittingness of Bill's betrayal. Given what she had been doing with Jim Feehan, cosmic justice called for a deed of equal weight on Bill's part. She knew she deserved this. Yet she was shocked and furious. Was this what the phrase a broken heart meant? She felt she had been cleft in two by her husband.

"What are you going to do?" Doris asked.

"I have half a mind to go and find myself a man."

Doris laughed nervously at this defiance and Agnes studied her reaction. She decided this was no time to confide in Doris about Jim Feehan. She doubted such a time would ever come. Far better to accept Doris's commiserations and act the role of the innocent and injured party.

Do? She hadn't the faintest idea what to do.

And that evening Jim called. Bill only mumbled when she said she was going to the library. Did he even care where she went or what she did? His indifference seemed to excuse her and condemn him. Ever since Bill had come home from the office she had been surreptitiously studying him. She had had no difficulty convincing herself that he was a stranger to her, someone she did not know and could not begin to understand.

The fact that Jim Feehan was half drunk made it easier to talk to him, though first she had to coax him out of his office and drive him to his apartment. He was in no condition to drive his own car. In his little kitchen she put on coffee and then, turning to him, let her eyes fill with tears and moved into his arms with a little cry.

"Hey, hey, what's this?"

She told him. There wasn't much to tell, but she could not tire of repeating the few facts she had. Her husband was unfaithful to her. He had been for years. With Phyllis O'Rourke Mackin. What was she going to do?

"Did he admit it?"

"I haven't mentioned it to him! What would I say? 'I know you've been sleeping with a client for years'?"

"How did you find out?"

"A friend."

"Oh, come on, Agnes. What was it, an anonymous phone call?"

"It was not. It was my best friend. You know her."

"Doris Hagstrom!"

"How did you guess?"

He shrugged. His eyes were clear now, focused, and he sipped his coffee. "I suppose some stranger told Doris."

"Why do you keep talking about strangers?"

"Agnes, my love, think of it. What do you have to go on?"

"I know it's true."

"How do you know it's true?"

She assumed what she thought of as her Clara Owens' expression. "I know."

"You're sure Doris is your friend? I mean, she wouldn't say something like this just to start trouble?"

Agnes was patient with him. He would be unable to understand real friendship. Once he must have, but had he had a real friend since Frank O'Rourke? Agnes trusted Doris. Of course she did.

"The person who told her is a young man doing research on Frank O'Rourke. You've met him. You suggested she contact him, for our book. Well, he certainly knew something we didn't. And it concerned Phyllis Mackin and my husband."

"Paul Gardiner."

She nodded. Jim seemed more shocked now than when she had first told him her news. No doubt it had taken time for the seriousness of what she was saying to sink in.

They sat on the couch, she accepted his offer of a

brandy, it went well with the coffee, and, far more sympathetic than before, he urged her to go over the whole story, again and again. How good it was to be cradled in his arms, to feel safe and protected, as she spoke of Bill's perfidy. Earlier she had thought her own conduct mitigated his. Now, as the depths of his treachery became clearer to her, it was her affair with Jim Feehan that seemed to right a balance.

"You mustn't tell your husband, you know," Jim said.

"How can I possibly keep silent?"

"Don't tell him." He held her tightly in his arms. They were standing at the door, as she prepared to go out to her car and drive back to her forever-sullied home. "Promise me you won't."

"He doesn't deserve my silence, Jim."

He agreed. "I'm thinking of you. Of what such a confrontation might do to you. You're not hard and callous, Clara."

A slip of the lip, but his calling her Clara did it. She promised not to talk to Bill about Phyllis O'Rourke Mackin. She would suffer in silence.

How odd that Jim should be relieved at her decision to spare herself the emotionally costly confrontation with her husband.

"Does he love me?" she wondered as she drove home. "Does Jim Feehan love me?"

And it seemed to her that he must. Could she possibly have an affair with a man who did not love her?

16

BILL FLOREY recognized the name Jim Feehan, but when his secretary identified his caller as the editor of the *Fox River Messenger* Sunday book page, he told her he definitely was out.

"Should I give him an appointment?"

Mrs. Ordway's pencil, poised at a 45° angle above her steno pad, seemed to invite mercy, bonhomie, general availability. But that way lay disaster. One did not run an efficient office on humanitarian principles. He did not propose to have the equivalent of the Statue of Liberty in his outer office: give me your tired, your poor. Besides, Feehan's connection suggested he was just another Frank O'Rourke freak. Bill Florey had made it an ironclad rule never to say a public word about his client at one remove. For him, Frank O'Rourke had been reduced to a legal and business problem and he was more than willing to leave the lofty speculations and appraisals to others.

"Try to avoid it," he told Mrs. Ordway. "If you can find out what he wants without appearing too interested, do it. But it's pretty obvious."

"What do you mean?"

"He's a journalist, Mrs. Ordway."

"He is also manager of the Pawnee branch of the Fox River Public Library." From Mrs. Ordway's lips this modest title emerged as some unimaginable apogee of accomplishment. "I have known him for years, Mr. Florey. If you want someone to vouch for the man."

"Mrs. Ordway, my wife knows the man too. I simply do not have the time."

He swiveled in his chair, writing finis to what threatened to evolve from minor interruption to noticeable annoyance. Mrs. Ordway covered the distance to the door soundlessly but he could have predicted to the split second her opening of the door. The door, having opened, would immediately close. But today, in a break of routine, the door did not close. There was a surprised cry from Mrs. Ordway. Bill Florey swung in his chair to see a tall, nervously smiling man approaching his desk.

"What the hell is this?"

"I'm sorry, Mr. Florey." Mrs. Ordway had scampered along at the intruder's side and now began to tug at his sleeve.

"My name is James Feehan."

"I don't give a damn what your name is. I won't have you . . ."

"I am an acquaintance of your wife."

It was the comic sight of Mrs. Ordway trying to pull Feehan toward the door that caused Bill Florey to relent. That and a minor curiosity about a man who had encouraged Agnes in her delusion that she could write.

"It's all right, Mrs. Ordway. Mr. Feehan has already disrupted my schedule."

Feehan seemed about to apologize for his manner of entry, but then did not. Without invitation, he took a chair across the desk from Florey. Mrs. Ordway actually shook her pencil at this impertinence. Turning to her employer, she launched into an abject apology, seeming to want to take back the mildly favorable things she had said of Feehan moments before. Florey dismissed her with a reassuring smile. She bore no responsibility for this curious librarian.

"I've come to blackmail you," Feehan said without preamble when the door had closed behind Mrs. Ordway.

Involuntarily, Florey stirred in his chair as, despite himself, his mind was flooded with dozens of deeds that might provide a basis for blackmail. After his surprising remark, Feehan smiled, his lips slowly assuming a curve before they parted and teeth appeared.

"Very effective," Florey said. "An opening remark worthy of your dramatic way of forcing your entrance."

"Thank you."

"What is it you want?"

"I want Frank O'Rourke's unfinished novel."

"I'm sure you do." Florey emitted a barking laugh. "This is why I would never have let you in. Have you any idea how many O'Rourke fans knock on my door?"

"I want it today," Feehan said, still smiling.

"If you're serious, you're crazy. Are you crazy?"

"No, merely desperate. I must have the manuscript."

"The answer, needless to say, is no."

"The answer is yes. Mr. Florey, perhaps you consider your affair with Mrs. Mackin your own business. Many friends and devotees of Frank O'Rourke might consider it a subtle form of exploitation. And your fellow lawyers might regard it as somewhat unprofessional."

"Get out of here." Florey stood, but Feehan remained

in his chair. He also retained what now was a most annoying smile. He must be mad, Florey thought.

"Of course it is your wife who would be hurt the most."

Florey sat down. He did not like to make decisions without considering a problem from all sides, and this problem had been dropped on him so suddenly and unexpectedly that he had no idea how to handle it. A precipitous decision would be all wrong. Call the police? Call in Fleischer, Fish, or Finn as witnesses? Humor Feehan until he had maneuvered the looney librarian into an exposed and vulnerable position? What? But sitting down again had been a decision in itself. He had already made a concession to Feehan.

It seemed to him, in the first flashing moment of reflection, that it was well he had not denied the basic charge. To ignore it was to treat it with contempt, although he did not doubt that his denial of such an affair with Phyllis would carry conviction. A lawyer must learn, if not to lie, then to tell half-truths as if they were the sum of the matter. Since the charge was true, the question became: How had Feehan learned of it?

His acquaintance with Agnes could scarcely explain his knowledge. He was threatening to inform Agnes. Bill Florey found that he was profoundly distressed by the thought of Agnes learning of his affair with Phyllis Mackin. For that matter, he would be embarrassed to have anyone know of it. After all, Phyllis was no longer young. She drank. The combination of the two put him in a bad light. He could not be thought to have been overwhelmed by her attractiveness and she could be imagined to be in a condition where her consent was less than conscious. But it was the imagined expression on Agnes's face if she learned of this that made Bill Florey go cold with dread. The strangest thing about this affair with Phyllis had been its surreal character.

That withdrawn silent house, with its lack of schedule,

its mistress who drank and kept the hours of a burglar, its master no longer master of himself yet swooshing about the house and grounds in a motorized wheelchair.

Emil. Emil knew. A week before, when Florey had emerged from Phyllis's bedroom, he had nearly fallen over Emil Mackin's wheelchair parked just outside the door. How long had he been there? The head lolled, drool ran from the corner of his mouth. But as his head rolled, one bloodshot eye caught Florey's and Florey felt momentarily like Captain Ahab confronting Moby Dick. Some whale, Emil, some driven fisherman himself. The incident had not bothered him. Poor dumb Emil. Even if the jelly in his skull could register the meaning of outside events, he could do nothing about them. So how had Feehan learned?

"You're guessing," Florey said. The remark was a mistake, a concessive remark.

"You know I'm not." Feehan turned didactic. "First, what I have said is true. Second, you do not want it known. Third, you will do as I say."

"The only point that makes sense is the second. I certainly do not want you going around making crazy claims."

"If they were crazy, you would already have telephoned the police. I am blackmailing you. That can only be effective if you are guilty."

"My present concern is to spare my wife the pain of hearing false and disturbing charges about me."

Feehan's smile was back. Florey would have given much for the chance to wipe it off that insolent face.

He said, "Who have you been talking to? Kevin?"

Feehan did not answer.

"It has to be Kevin or Hermie."

Feehan lifted his brow and tipped his head in a mute No comment.

"Why the hell don't you just steal the goddam manuscript yourself? Why bring me into it?"

Feehan stood. "I want it tonight."

"That's impossible."

"I want it tonight." Feehan considered his watch. "I will telephone you at this office at nine o'clock."

"I can't get it for you today."

"At nine o'clock. There will be no delays. If I do not have that manuscript in my hands by nine-fifteen, I will make known the manner in which you have been servicing your client, Mrs. Phyllis O'Rourke Mackin."

Feehan turned and walked rapidly to the door. He did not look back before letting himself out. The door opened again immediately and Mrs. Ordway came in, but Florey waved her back out. He had to think. It was inconceivable that O'Rourke's unfinished novel should be handed over like this, on demand, without possibility of reprisal. It was particularly undesirable that it should simply disappear, without evidence of a theft, without a finger pointing elsewhere than at those in whose custody the manuscript was—notably among them, Mr. William Florey, attorney at law.

17

THE BODY of Mrs. Emil Mackin, nee Phyllis O'Rourke, was found floating face down in the swimming pool of her home at 10:30 in the morning by the mailman.

"I thought she was doing the dead man's float," the mailman said to Captain Phil Keegan.

"Was she often in the pool when you brought the mail?"

"Never. That always struck me. A wonderful pool like this and no one ever in it. Not when I delivered mail, anyway. Of course, that's in the morning. But you'd think once in a while there'd be someone using the damned thing. How much do you suppose it costs just to run the filter? A pretty penny, you can bet."

His name was Chet Bigelow and he was understandably nervous and inclined to babble. Even so, Phil Keegan didn't much care for the mailman. His short-sleeved blue shirt was heavily starched and the scrawny arms and scrawnier neck emerging from the unwrinkleable confines of the shirt gave Bigelow the aspect of a turtle. Some crustacean or other. But what really bothered Keegan was that Phyllis's body had had to wait until ten in the morning and the arrival of the mailman in order to be discovered.

He looked around for Horvath. There were things to be done, rounding up the household for questioning, getting the medical examiner here so the body could be moved and they could proceed with some idea as to times, causes, and the like. Meanwhile, he had Chet Bigelow.

"So you were surprised to see someone in the pool?"

Bigelow had a thin face distributed unevenly on either side of a narrow sharp nose. His eyebrows lifted expressively. "You saw how she was dressed. At first I thought it was a bathing suit."

"What was it?" Keegan asked, not for information, but to see where the question might take Bigelow.

"Don't you know?"

"Describe it to me."

"She was in her goddam underwear. Panties. A bra."

"I see."

"You asked me, Captain, and I answered. Don't act as if I'm some kind of peeping Tom."

"How long did it take before you decided she wasn't doing the dead man's float?"

They were standing on a flagstone patio that overlooked the pool. Behind them French doors opened into the den. Bigelow brought out a pocket watch, reeling it in as if it were a goldfish. When he pressed the stem, it flew open.

"Eleven-o-two," he said. "I've got to get going, Captain."

"You're not going anywhere."

"But I've got mail to deliver."

"Call up and get a substitute. We need your help here."

Bigelow was flattered by this. They were joined by Cy Horvath, who looked at Bigelow with Slavic impassivity. Keegan had seen Horvath's unreadable expression elicit more response than a string of questions and he himself was still unsure whether Horvath's manner was deliberate or simply the way he was. Maybe it was both. In any case, Keegan would not have wanted to get along without Cy Horvath. Bigelow's manner wilted in Horvath's presence and he turned and hurried into the house to make his phone call.

"The medical examiner is on his way," Horvath said.

"Bennett?"

"No, Phelps."

Keegan groaned. Phelps moved with glacial slowness and his judgments were so cautious as to lose the name of judgment. Any hope that they would get a quick horseback estimate on time and cause of death disappeared with Phelps on the case.

"What about the house, Cy?"

"It's hard to say. Those doors were open, but that's probably how she left the house."

"In her underwear?"

"Her robe is by the pool."

"A robe."

"No, hers. The cook says it's hers."

"Where the hell was he all morning while she was floating in the pool?"

"In bed. If you can believe him, they keep pretty weird hours around here. His name is Kevin." Horvath's lower lip caught between his teeth briefly when he pronounced the v in Kevin. Keegan saw what he meant.

"There's a yardman too, Cy. Herman. He lives over the garage."

"The house may have been gone through, but it's hard to say until we know how neat a housekeeper she was."

"Where's the husband? Mr. Mackin?"

Horvath looked blankly at Keegan.

"He's had a stroke. He's in a wheelchair."

"That's her husband?"

"Then you've seen him." Keegan found that he was relieved. For a moment he had wondered if there might be another body in the pool.

"Kevin calls him the Blob. He also says she drank. Think that might be it?"

"What do you mean?"

"She has too much, wanders outside, and falls in the pool."

Keegan frowned. He did not like to imagine what might have happened. Horvath knew it was bad procedure. It was always better to keep the mind a blank. Theories were more often an impediment than a help. If there was any mystery here it would be solved by something a lot less impressive than a theory.

"Let's wait for Phelps, Cy."

But God only knew when Phelps would decide when death had occurred and how long the body had been in the pool. The body. He had to think of her this way. He had to crowd from his mind that Phyllis O'Rourke was dead. Frank dead, and now Phyllis. He had the wintry thought that, like Job's servant, he alone had escaped to report disasters that had befallen.

"Get the yardman, Cy. I'm going inside."

But, for a moment, neither man moved. Both stared at the point where the body, covered with a blanket, had been left after Phyllis had been declared dead. There had been no point in bundling her into the ambulance that had responded to Bigelow's frantic call. The call had brought Keegan as well. Keegan felt he was waking Phyllis and that it would be wrong to leave her lying there beside the pool, unattended.

Horvath went off then, through the trellised archway into the yard beyond the pool. It was than that Emil Mackin wheeled out of the house and came to a stop beside Keegan. Keegan lay a hand on Emil's shoulder, but the head with its wild sprouts of white hair continued its mad gyrations. Emil seemed to be humming. Was he trying to talk? It was an odd thought that he knew what had happened to Phyllis and would never be able to communicate it. But it was doubtful that Emil even realized he had become a widower. He had become a vegetable first and so was spared anything like grief.

Keegan began to turn the wheelchair back toward the house, but Emil hit the power switch and started off, circling the pool toward the driveway. Keegan watched him go, shaking his own head. It was a miracle that Emil had not long since sailed into the street and been hit by a car. Or gone over the steep bank at the far end of the yard that fell away to the river.

"Drunks and fools," he murmured, then wished he hadn't. As Cy had learned, Phyllis had a drinking problem. It was a damned shame Roger Dowling had not gotten to know her long ago.

Someone tugged at Keegan's sleeve. It was Bigelow, the mailman.

"I called in, Captain. Someone will be here to complete my deliveries."

"Good."

"The press has arrived," Bigelow said importantly. "I suppose they'll have to interview me."

"There are three of them," a patrolman who had come

outside told Keegan. The officer's name was Oyler and he was escorting Phelps to poolside. Keegan greeted the medical examiner and Phelps, a thick man with laid-back ears, nodded in reply. To say Good Morning would have been to put himself out on a meteorological limb. After all, what did he know of weather? Oyler led Phelps to the body and pulled back the blanket. The medical examiner had trouble getting his glasses on because of his ears but then, with great deliberation, he began to scrutinize the mortal remains of Phyllis O'Rourke Mackin. Keegan's stomach tightened at the sight of the lifeless face of the woman he had visited regularly, out of a sense of duty. He looked now on the face of a departed friend and the recognition did not even surprise him. Phelps seemed on the verge of concluding that this was, for purposes of these proceedings, a human body. Keegan told Bigelow to take a seat and left the mailman perched on the edge of a white wrought-iron chair staring popeyed across the pool at Phelps at work.

Keegan had expected to find Mervel and Ninian inside, but the third man was a stranger.

"Feehan? Who are you?"

"*Fox River Messenger.*"

"Mervel is the *Messenger.*"

"I'm an editor."

Even without Ninian's reaction, Keegan was unlikely to be impressed by that title. Editor of what? There was the society editor, Flo Eberle. There was the sports editor, who was an ass, always badmouthing the Cubs. There was the political editor who was a second cousin of the Pianones. It turned out that Feehan was editor of the Sunday book page.

"So how's it by you, Keegan?" Ninian said. "Where's the corpus delicious?"

"You're editor of the book page?" Keegan said to Feehan.

Feehan was tall, about Keegan's age; a bit of a pot, but his face was smooth and his hair, worn long, was graying in a somewhat theatrical way. Feehan had a way of defensively tilting his chin that Keegan seemed to remember.

"Feehan. Jim Feehan?"

"That's right. I knew Frank and Phyllis. I knew you too. As far back as Saint Hilary's grade school."

"Jim Feehan. But you're a librarian."

"I'm also editor of the *Fox River Messenger* Sunday book page. You realize that Mrs. Emil Mackin is Phyllis O'Rourke, Frank O'Rourke's sister. Frank O'Rourke, our old schoolmate and later famous novelist. Hence, book page."

Feehan's smile seemed meant to urge Keegan through the steps of this impressionistic argument. Keegan remembered Feehan now, remembered him as a pain in the neck. At high school dances, Feehan and his partner always ended up being surrounded by spectators admiring them as they did to perfection whatever the latest dance happened to be.

"Since when do librarians and/or book-page editors chase ambulances?"

Mervel said, "How do you classify it, Keegan? Homicide, murder, suicide, what?"

"I don't classify it. The medical examiner and the prosecutor classify it. I just do what I'm told."

Ninian snickered appreciatively. "Sure you do. So do we. How did she die?"

"The body was found in the pool."

"Drowned." Ninian and Mervel were taking notes. Feehan stood there with his mouth slack. You would have thought he was the next of kin. Hadn't Frank O'Rourke disliked Feehan? It seemed to Keegan he had. Certainly Phyllis hadn't liked him. What the hell was he doing here?

"The body was found in the pool," Keegan repeated carefully.

Two pencils poised over their pages. "You saying she was dead when she was thrown into the pool?"

Keegan laughed mirthlessly. "You guys. Look, the body was found in the pool. She was dead."

"Who found it?"

"The mailman."

"Name?"

"Chet Bigelow. He's out by the pool. Why don't you talk to him? Just don't bother Phelps. He's slow enough as it is."

Ninian and Mervel were content to be diverted to Bigelow, but Feehan stayed.

"You remember me, don't you, Phil?"

Keegan nodded.

"You people wouldn't be here if her death was accidental, would you?"

Keegan looked at him, then thought, what the hell. "It may have been an accident and it may not have been."

"Keegan, I knew her. You did too, I know that, maybe better than I did. But do you realize how vulnerable she was?"

"How so?"

"Think about it. Frank was a famous writer. His fame came largely after he died, but it is widespread. People are interested in every aspect of his life. Collectors are after anything they can lay their hands on. They descend on Fox River like vultures. Believe me, I know."

"You have some letters of Frank's, don't you?"

"I'm surprised you know that." And Feehan's expression matched his words.

"Phyllis mentioned it. I have a letter myself."

"Hang on to it. Anyway, Phyllis won't give the time of day to Frank's fans, she won't talk to them, she won't release all the papers and documents she has—you know, let scholars use them. And then, as if to enrage them further, she announces there's an unfinished novel."

"Announces?"

"Well, it got out. People learned of it. She had to know they would. Can you begin to imagine what an item like that is worth?"

"How much?"

Feehan flipped his hands helplessly in answer. "There's a young man prowling around town right now who strikes me as absolutely ruthless."

"Why?"

"He's a collector. But not just an ordinary O'Rourke buff. This guy's different. He claimed to be on the faculty of Northwestern. He isn't. I checked. Then he said he was a Chicago lawyer. Again, false."

"What's his name?"

"He calls himself Paul Gardiner."

"That's not his name?"

"Who knows?"

"Where's he staying?"

Feehan didn't know. Could he describe the man? The description was imprecise and Feehan seemed to realize it.

"Look, Mervel and Ninian would be better at that sort of thing. They saw this fellow, in the Foxy Lounge. I had a drink with Paul Gardiner there, and Mervel and Ninian were in the place at the time."

"Paul Gardiner," Keegan mused, trying the name.

They fell silent then. The body was being taken away, in a bag, the burden swinging irreverently between two of Phelps's assistants. Keegan looked at Feehan to see how the self-styled friend of the family was reacting. The librarian backed away, to allow plenty of room for the procession to pass. He looked more frightened than sad.

Phelps came up to Keegan, wringing his hands like Pontius Pilate. Keegan's watch read 11:45.

"Doctor, Lieutenant Horvath will take the information from you, all right? Here he comes now."

Cy had just returned through the trellised archway. Beside him walked a slight bearded man, Herman, who took care of the grounds. Keegan took Cy aside.

"I'm going to catch the noon Mass at Saint Hilary's, Cy. See what Phelps has found out. That fellow with him is named Feehan. He's playing newspaperman. Find out what everybody was doing and when. You know. Why the hell does it take an ambulance siren to wake this house up?"

Horvath nodded. Keegan lifted a hand in greeting to Herman.

The yardman brought a gloved hand to his forehead in mock salute.

Keegan left. Things were in competent hands with Cy. There was no reason not to go to Roger Dowling's 12:00 Mass.

He would say a prayer for Phyllis.

He was ashamed that it had taken him this long to think to ask peace for her soul. But then, it had taken her death to make him realize she was a dear friend and not merely the sister of Frank O'Rourke.

18

MARIE Murkin was not unused to the idea of death. As house-keeper of the St. Hilary parish rectory, she seldom saw a week go by without a funeral. That might have been high frequency for your average parish, but the age level of those still living within the boundaries of St. Hilary's was higher than average.

Mrs. Murkin could remember the parish when the school had been a flourishing affair, her own day measured in part by its bells and recess periods. And of course the pastor had been involved in the school, teaching religion classes. Showing the flag, Monsignor Hunniker used to call it. Monsignor Hunniker had always been a little wary of the nuns, as if they might be plotting a take-over of the parish. Some years later such fears might have been justified, but in those long-ago days, during what Mrs. Murkin sometimes thought of as the Golden Age of St. Hilary's, the nuns had been a docile lot, if anything too respectful of Monsignor Hunniker, who was, if the truth be told, a bit of a bully.

He had had weights and springs and pulleys and other instruments of strenuous exercise in the basement and he had looked the fittest of humans. He had golfed and bowled as well as shown the flag frequently on the playground of the parish school, hitting long fly balls to the amazement of the kids. And he had been felled by a stroke at an early age.

Father Dowling had been quite a change from Monsignor Hunniker, and at first Marie Murkin had doubted that the quiet pipe-smoking pensive priest would do. But he had grown on her as he had on the parish and he was now the object of her fiercest loyalty. She had some notion of what the man had been through. It was difficult to think of a priest as the victim of the drink, difficult unless one had been a parish housekeeper as long as Marie Murkin. Some of Monsignor Hunniker's poker parties had gone on into the wee hours and there was more than one blurred eye and fuzzy tongue when they called it quits. Those invited to the game were invited to spend the night as well, and it was a good thing. They were in no condition to drive after they had cashed in their chips. But that had been a special thing and it never really got out of hand. However, Father Dowling had had to spend some time in a sanitarium. His gentleness could be explained, she supposed, by the fact that he had been on the bottom himself. And that gave him an uncanny ability to assess people too. He was seldom fooled by anyone, certainly not for long. If he had any fault, it was his tendency to tease. For example, the way he spoke of Mrs. Mackin as her rival.

"Maybe Phil confuses your names," he suggested, a twinkle in his eye.

"I wouldn't know about that."

"I don't want you to be jealous, Marie. You can't expect Captain Keegan to rush into marriage. He was married once before, you know."

"So was I."

The reminder had taken the playfulness out of the pastor's manner, but wasn't it like him to have noticed her interest in Phil Keegan? "Interest" might be too strong a word, or it might be too weak, to describe the feelings she had for the pastor's friend. It seemed to Marie Murkin that she and Captain Keegan saw eye to eye on things. They were at ease with each other. She always made sure he had a fresh bottle of beer when he was playing cribbage with Father Dowling or when the two men were proving once again that the Chicago Cubs were unworthy of their fans. Father Dowling, not drinking himself, was apt to forget to keep his guest supplied. Cooking was a more exciting task when she knew Captain Keegan would be there, but just as often he ate at the rectory without forewarning, so she could cook with the thought that he *might* be sharing the food with Father Dowling. She always prepared twice as much as Father Dowling was likely to eat. Captain Keegan made up for that. When he came. She would never have admitted it, but Marie Murkin felt a twinge of disappointment whenever Captain Keegan was not at table with the pastor. It was a fairly good bet he would have lunch with Father Dowling, attending the noon Mass as often as he did and afterward stopping by the sacristy to say hello. What could be more natural than that Father Dowling should ask him back for lunch?

"I realize what an imposition on you this is, Marie," Father Dowling said once. "If you'd rather not have me spring guests on you without warning, just say the word."

"You're the pastor, Father Dowling, and your table is your table."

"But you're the one who has to prepare the meals."

"Have you heard me complain?"

"No, I haven't. You haven't said a thing. Even so . . ."

"When I have a complaint, you'll know about it, Father

Dowling. To tell you the truth, it's a joy to see a man with the appetite of Captain Keegan."

And that was when he began to tease her. Perhaps he would never have continued if she hadn't actually blushed, and at her age, thereby indicating she did indeed regard Captain Keegan with some interest. After all these years of waiting on priests, people seemed to think she was some kind of nun, but she had human feelings, she was still a woman with life in her, and however unsatisfactory her marriage had been, it had had its good moments. Marie Murkin could think pleasantly of the consolations of marriage. Why shouldn't she be attracted by the thought of having a man like Philip Keegan to take care of her, particularly after all these years of looking after herself?

"I'll never say a word to Captain Keegan," Father Dowling said, and for once she hoped he was fibbing.

"This Mackin woman is a childhood friend, is that it?"

"Well, the sister of a childhood friend."

"Older or younger?"

"Than whom?"

"The childhood friend."

"I don't know." He drew on his pipe, eyes twinkling. "About your age, I'd say."

But whenever Captain Keegan mentioned visiting Mrs. Mackin he made it sound like a chore.

"Why do you have to?" Mrs. Murkin asked, assuming she was not excluded from the exchange. "Doesn't she have any family?"

"Her husband is gaga and her brother is dead."

"No children?"

Captain Keegan shook his head. He couldn't talk because his mouth was full of food.

"What about in-laws?"

Keegan finished chewing. "The Mackins? I don't know. He wasn't from here, originally."

"I meant her brother's wife."

"Wives. There were three."

Mrs. Murkin made a reproving sound, and she meant Mrs. Mackin to be one of its targets.

"How many husbands has *she* had?" she asked sweetly.

Captain Keegan frowned and she regretted the question. "Only one."

"There's more gravy," she said brightly. "I'll get it."

And now today, having seen Captain Keegan park his car and go into the church for the noon Mass, Marie Murkin, humming, began to prepare lunch for two. She turned on the radio to catch the news and a moment later her humming stopped.

She turned up the volume and listened carefully. She had two thoughts. How odd it was that Captain Keegan should come to Mass today. And, second, that the woman Father Dowling had called her rival was no more.

19

PHIL KEEGAN liked to talk with Roger Dowling about the case he was working on, particularly when he could start with something as startling as a body floating in a swimming pool. But this time it was different, this time it had been an old and dear friend of his, and he could count on Roger Dowling to see the difference.

"Thank God you went to see her, Roger."

Roger Dowling said nothing. Well, it had been a forlorn try, but one Keegan did not regret having made. He could not help wondering how Phyllis had stood spiritually, religiously, and it would be good to know if Father Dowling had brought her back to the faith of her childhood, maybe even heard her confession. But Roger could not tell him that sort of thing. Keegan decided he would simply assume it had happened like that. But he could not convince himself of it. He fell silent over lunch.

"She hadn't been to church in years, Roger."

The priest nodded.

"I'm not excusing her, but what the hell, look at all the people who don't take the Sunday obligation seriously anymore. Who can blame them, the way these theologians talk? You've heard it more than I have, Roger. They really believe it doesn't matter. They go when they feel like it and they don't feel like it very often. Given the advice they get, who can say they're wrong?"

"The theologians are wrong."

"Sure they are. But your average Catholic isn't going to take on the job of deciding which theologian to listen to. If a man is a priest and maybe a professor too and he speaks of going to Mass on Sunday as something a person might or might not decide to do, well, people are going to listen to him and take the easier way. I don't blame them."

"You don't follow that kind of advice, Phil."

"Well, no, I don't. But I could." He sounded unconvincing to himself. "What do I know? I'm just a dumb cop."

"Don't worry about your friend, Phil . . ."

"Do you mean that?" Keegan asked, his voice lifting.

"I'm speaking quite generally. You and I can't measure the divine mercy. God isn't a cop."

Keegan frowned. "He is a judge."

"More like counsel for the defense."

It wasn't much consolation, but it was some. At his age, Keegan was not unfamiliar with the death of friends, but the fact that in the line of duty he encountered more than his share of deaths did not make it easier to face the fact that Phyllis O'Rourke was dead.

"You don't think it was an accident, Phil?"

"No."

"I got the impression she never used the pool."

"She didn't mean to use it this time." Keegan's eyes slid

toward Mrs. Murkin, who had paused on her way back to the kitchen. "She was wearing underwear when she was found, not a bathing suit."

"What does the medical examiner say?"

"Nothing yet. It's Phelps."

"Even Phelps should have something to say by now. When was the body found?"

"Hours ago. I'll call out there when we finish lunch."

"Why don't we just go out?"

Keegan smiled. "Okay."

There was seldom any need to explain the presence of a priest on any scene that required the police, and Roger Dowling, thank God, was unmistakably a priest. Whatever the reluctance of his fellow clerics to appear in the traditional priestly garb, Roger Dowling always wore a black suit, rabat, and Roman collar. It pleased Keegan to think that the clergy, like the police, wore uniforms.

"You don't wear one, Phil."

"You know what I mean."

"Maybe if you thought of all those other priests as plain-clothes men."

A kidder. Roger Dowling had always been a gentle kidder, not enough to hurt your feelings, just enough to help you keep your perspective. Why the hell should Phil Keegan work himself into a sweat because some priests chose to dress like bums or male models or whatever?

At the house Horvath told him it was Phelps's judgment that the victim had been struck on the head and dumped into the pool.

"The blow to the head came first, anyway."

"She didn't have to be struck? Did Phelps say that?"

But the precision was Horvath's. The suggestion was that Phyllis could have tripped, struck her head, and fallen unconscious into the pool. Maybe. Meanwhile Keegan wanted to question the household.

"I'll look around, Phil," Roger Dowling said.

"Suit yourself." But Keegan was a little disappointed. He had assumed Roger had come to watch him in action.

The cook, Kevin, was hysterical with grief. He was, as Horvath had suggested, more than a little effeminate, but Keegan could attest to his wizardry in the kitchen.

"I simply cannot believe it, Captain Keegan. That wonderful vital woman, gone."

"The medical examiner doubts her death was accidental."

"Of course it wasn't! Mrs. Mackin was not likely to walk inadvertently into the pool."

"Maybe she went for a swim."

"Ha. You knew her. She hated to swim."

"Why the pool? I never understood that."

"It was his idea. Before. She actually talked of having it filled in, because of the mister. If anyone were to fall into the pool and drown, you'd bet it would be him." Kevin spoke almost wistfully. No doubt it irked him to realize that the pathetic drooling man was all the employer he had left. Which suggested he might soon be out of a job.

"A cook is never out of a job for long," Kevin said smugly. "But I will miss her. She drank too much and we know what that does to the taste buds, let alone the appetite, but she did appreciate a well-prepared meal, no matter how little of it she might eat."

"What did she have last night?"

"Beef stroganoff."

"What's in that?"

Kevin sighed, ticking off the ingredients. The list matched more or less the one Phelps had provided. Her last meal had been last night. The estimate of time of death was midnight to three in the morning.

"Did she eat alone last night?"

"Oh no. We all ate together, as usual."

"We?"

"Phyllis—Mrs. Mackin—the husband, Herman, and myself."

"You called her Phyllis?"

"Not to her face, no. But this was a very informal house. You must have noticed that when you visited."

"As a matter of fact, I didn't."

Kevin shrugged. "I thought detectives noticed *every*-thing."

"Only what we're not supposed to. After she ate, what?"

"She took the Blob out for a walk, and then . . ."

"The Blob is Mr. Mackin?"

"That's right. She was touchingly devoted to him."

This was another thing Keegan had not noticed on his visits. Phyllis had scarcely mentioned her husband to him. Not that he blamed her. What could she say? It was a little unnerving to hear the whir of that motorized chair and turn to see the lolling head of Emil Mackin, saliva running freely from the corner of his mouth as he tried unsuccessfully to focus his gaze.

"He must run into a lot of things with that chair."

"You'd be surprised. But, as I say, if anyone was to fall into the pool, you'd think it would be the Blob."

"You think she fell into the pool?"

"I do *not*. It could not have been an accident. She never used the damned pool and she's found floating in it wearing panties and a bra?"

"She drank."

"Sure she did. Lots. And she was not a modest woman.

It was a hot night, she was half snaffled, she stepped out of her robe."

"You saw her do this?"

"Not last night. I'm imagining. But I've seen her get comfortable and to hell with anyone who might be looking on." Kevin looked sharply at Keegan and said. "Was she assaulted?"

"Sexually? No."

"Some other way?"

"Was anyone else here last night?"

"Florey, the lawyer, was here for a time. But he left early."

"When's early?"

"Eight, nine, something like that. You think someone attacked her and threw her into the pool?"

"Anyone else beside Florey?"

Kevin shook his head impatiently.

"Tell me about the mailman."

"The mailman! Ol' Popeye? What a creep. Do you know, he would leave that silly ass-backward vehicle of his at the foot of the driveway and come sneaking up here on his crepe soles? He was dying to get a peek."

"At Mrs. Mackin?"

"I told you she threw modesty to the winds when she wanted to be comfortable."

"How old would you say she was?"

Kevin cocked his head and smirked. "You think too old? Don't kid yourself. How old is Popeye? She would have looked pretty good to him."

"How about you?"

Kevin ran his tongue around inside his mouth and then, giving Keegan his profile, said, "I found her as attractive as I do any woman."

"Do you live in the house?"

"I do. I have a little suite just behind the kitchen. Want to see it?"

"Later."

"Any time."

Before talking with Herman, Keegan called in Cy and told him about Florey's presence in the house the previous evening.

"Where's Roger Dowling?"

"He left. Said he didn't want to get in the way. Talked to Mervel. Looked around the pool and strolled around the yard a bit first."

Did that mean Roger was guessing Phyllis's death was an accident? Well, he could be right. But Captain Phil Keegan did not think so.

20

"THE JACKPOT," Flo Eberle said without preamble.

Father Dowling took the phone from his ear and stared
at it. He knew that a certain Chicago radio station made ran-
dom phone calls which, if answered by "WMAQ is going to
make me rich" won the caller a jackpot. He decided against
hanging up.

"This is Roger Dowling."

"I know, I know. Your hunch was right. About Paul
Gardiner."

"Is this Flo Eberle?"

A pause. "Yes, this is Flo Eberle. You do remember
coming to see me, don't you?"

He placated her. How could he ever forget his visit? He
thought of that long corridor with its open doors and the smiling malevolent rivals of the entertainment editor.

"She thinks she's in Show Biz," Mervel had told Father Dowling with contempt. "She really believes she's a friend of the stars. Maybe she even thinks she is one."

"Wouldn't that help her work?"

"It doesn't help her *at* work."

Now, on the phone, Roger Dowling could appreciate the reactions of Flo Eberle's cohorts. Why on earth would she assume that he would immediately recognize her voice? But she had called to do him a favor and he was grateful.

"You have to promise to keep it under your hat, or whatever. I want an exclusive."

"Of course."

Her voice dropped. He could imagine her cupping the phone and darting glances at her bank of television sets. He closed his eyes as she talked and felt again an almost-forgotten vertigo. It was like an interrogatory in the diocesan marriage court. The excited lilt in Flo Eberle's voice did little to diminish the sadness he felt in listening to her; rather, it increased it.

"That isn't his true name, then?"

"Sure it is. His legal name, anyway. The second husband adopted him. His name was Gardiner."

"But the woman, the second wife of Frank O'Rourke?"

"Is now named Pizarro? Right. She shuffled off Gardiner years ago."

"Didn't Gardiner adopt both the boys?"

"He did. The other one, the one who was killed, changed his name back to O'Rourke. Legally."

Roger Dowling hummed in response, as if to keep Flo Eberle on key.

"The other, Paul Gardiner, managed a driving range in Orange County until a month or so ago. You know what a driving range is?"

Roger Dowling smiled. "Yes. I suppose you'll delay writing the story now."

"Why the heck would I delay?" The profanity had been emended in midair.

It seemed presumptuous, asking a newspaperwoman if she had heard the news. She had, but had made no connection with the research she had so successfully completed. "Aunt Phyllis," she murmured. "I wonder if he knew her."

"Did you get a California address and telephone number for Paul Gardiner?"

"Uh uh. Not even for you, Father. I don't want to lead you into temptation. You try to get in touch with him and the next thing I know, I'm scooped."

"Was he in California when you tracked him down?"

But Flo was through giving information. She sounded as if she now regretted having made the call. "Tell me, Father, what is your interest in Paul Gardiner?"

"I told you."

"Remind me. I've forgotten."

"His parents were married in my church."

"But what . . ."

He left it there. Let her think it was some professional caution on his part to balance her own unwillingness to say where in California Paul Gardiner could now be reached.

"What makes you think he's in California?" Phil Keegan asked.

Keegan sat in a leather chair in Father Dowling's den, a glass of beer in his hand. Marie Murkin, in the doorway, turned. She had just left a fresh bottle of beer for Phil.

"Isn't that the man who came here about getting married?"

"Paul Gardiner was here?"

"Ask Marie, Phil."

Marie Murkin, her hand over her mouth, looked abjectly at Roger Dowling. She was sorry to have said it but he really did not blame her. After all, what secrets did they have from Captain Keegan? And it had been Phil who brought up the name of Paul Gardiner in the course of a résumé of his new case he had been giving Roger Dowling.

"I'm sorry, Father," Mrs. Murkin said.

"You're sorry," Keegan groused. "How do you think we feel? What was he doing here?"

Marie left. Roger Dowling busied himself with his pipe. A moment later, through clouds of smoke, he said, "It still seems strange that the body had to await discovery by the mailman at after ten o'clock in the morning."

The body had been found on Wednesday. Today was Friday and little more was known now than on the morning the body was discovered.

"Oh, we know lots of things," Keegan corrected. "What we don't know is if they tell us anything about how Phyllis died."

"Then it could still be an accident?"

Keegan frowned. "It can't be completely excluded. Her blood was full of alcohol, but I suppose it always was. She could have fallen, hit her head, rolled into the pool."

"Hit her head on what?"

"The tile, the ladder. Roger, water sloshes over the side of the pool all the time. It would be a miracle if we found what she struck her head on."

"If she did."

"Yeah. And there were bruises above her knees, too. Here. On both legs. Phelps thinks they are recent. What caused them? We don't know. Of course, a body bears all kinds of marks. . . ." Phil let it go. "What doesn't make sense is the way she was dressed. I mean, in her skivvies."

"You don't credit Kevin?"

"That she ran around in little or nothing? Roger, it wasn't that warm a night."

"Tell me about Tuesday night. Who was there, at the house? The time of death is thought to be midnight?"

"Not earlier than midnight." Keegan raised his eyes. "Phelps."

"So it could have been later?"

"Personally, I would put it closer to three, something like that. Bennett agrees."

"Ah." Bennett was Phelps's superior, an efficient man who had made an art of the macabre. His assessments were swift and sure and, as far as one could see, dispassionate. Had he ever been upset by the sight of a corpse? Phelps, for all his phlegm, had apparently gone from poolside into the Mackin house to be sick in the bathroom.

"He told Horvath he was lucky to get through medical school. Did you know each med student gets his own corpse to dissect? They keep them in formaldahyde and . . ."

Keegan, riding the waves of the restorative beers he had drunk, pursued this diverting if ghoulish bit of information.

Roger Dowling felt not guilt, but a slight uneasiness at his silence about the connection of Paul Gardiner to Phyllis Mackin. After all, he had given his word to Flo Eberle. Besides, if she could go in search of the children of Frank O'Rourke and come up with Paul Gardiner, the police, in checking out Paul Gardiner, should be able to come up with the son of Frank O'Rourke. God knew enough people were pointing them in the direction of Paul Gardiner.

"Did you enjoy your talk with Herman, Phil?"

"Horvath did."

"What does Cy think?"

"Oh, he's telling the truth. They all sleep till noon every day, I'd bet on it. Herman had instructions not to raise a racket before then, so he just stayed in his apartment over the garage. I know for a fact that Phyllis did not like to greet the dawn. But she was usually awake by midmorning."

"While the cook slept on?"

Keegan shrugged. "She took care of Emil."

"How is he reacting to his wife's death?"

"He isn't. He's really out of it, Roger."

"What exactly is wrong with him?"

"Didn't you see him?"

"Oh, I got an idea of his condition. But what is the medical description of it?"

Keegan looked at the foam in his glass, puffing out his lower lip. He tipped his head to one side. "I don't know."

"Can he get up by himself? Does he put himself to bed?"

Phil did not like the question. Mainly because he did not know the answer. Roger Dowling was willing to bet Cy Horvath did, and that would excuse Phil. With Cy as his assistant, he didn't have to do everything himself.

"He sure gets around," Roger Dowling said.

"Yeah."

"Everything all right in here?" It was Marie Murkin, chirping in the doorway. She came in and took Keegan's empty bottle.

"Another?"

"No. No thanks, Marie."

"What exactly did Feehan say about Paul Gardiner?" Roger Dowling asked after Marie had said good night and gone off to bed. "Are the letters he received from Frank O'Rourke missing?"

"It's the diary that's missing. From the bookstore that used to be the O'Rourke residence. Those people, the Mosses, are sure Paul Gardiner took it. Well, kind of sure. He is when she isn't and vice versa." Keegan stood and shook his head as if to clear it. "You'll want to be turning in."

"Don't rush off on my account."

Phil looked at his empty glass, as if he regretted refusing Marie Murkin's offer of another bottle. Roger Dowling said nothing. If Phil asked for another, fine, but he was certainly not going to urge another on him. He remembered how innocent he himself had felt, in his drinking days, when someone offered him a drink, as if responsibility had passed to other shoulders.

Phil decided to go. When he had driven off, Roger Dowling locked up, but he went back to the den rather than to his room. He had finished his office for the day, had anticipated Matins and Lauds for the following day. He relit his pipe and looked at the cabinets where the parish records were kept. The volume in which the wedding of Paul O'Rourke and Lorraine Dolan was recorded had been the one Paul Gardiner wanted to see. Why would he want to take it?

How had he gotten in, and when?

The thought of someone entering the house, prowling about, taking things, perhaps at night while he slept, perhaps during the day when he was out and Mrs. Murkin on some errand, angered Roger Dowling. In either case, entry would have to be forced. To have one's own space invaded was violence indeed.

The only thing that told against Paul Gardiner as the thief was the fact that he had misrepresented his interest.

Apparently he had made no bones about his interest in the diary at Reading Matters, nor, if Feehan could be believed, about his interest in O'Rourke's letters. His father's letters. Was Gardiner driven by some odd piety to collect whatever belonged to his father or concerned him in any way? But, in that case, would he not, as his brother had done, resume his father's name? Whatever his motives, Paul Gardiner had come to Fox River because his father had once lived here. Now a diary was missing and a volume of the St. Hilary parish records. Did Feehan still have his letters? Most important of all, was the unfinished novel, the work on which Frank O'Rourke had been engaged when he died and which had been in his sister's possession, missing?

Phil Keegan did not have the answer to that question. He planned to talk it over with her lawyer in the morning.

"Lawyer?"

"He managed her brother's literary effects. William Florey."

21

TRUE to his word, Feehan telephoned Bill Florey at nine o'clock Tuesday night.

"Well?"

"I don't have it."

There was only silence on the line.

"Feehan, I don't have it because it isn't there."

"Where is it?"

How could he convince Feehan that there was no unfinished novel? Bill Florey could not imagine. At the moment, the threat of Agnes finding out about Phyllis seemed infinitely less menacing than it had when Feehan burst into his office. But it would not stop with Agnes learning of it.

He said now, playing for time, "It isn't where it is supposed to be."

"It has to be there. Didn't she keep everything in the house?"

"Yes. Yes, she did." He sensed that trying to divert Feehan with a lie about a cache of O'Rourke goodies elsewhere, with the much-desired unfinished novel among them, would not work.

"Why in hell didn't you keep looking for it?"

"Because you were going to telephone!"

He gained the advantage with that reminder and, with it, thought of a way out. What did Feehan know of O'Rourke's unpublished stuff, the rejected stories, the stories begun but never completed? Good God, he could fob off anything on the librarian as the start of a new O'Rourke novel.

"Go back and get it," Feehan said.

"This time I'll call you. I take it your number's in the book."

"I'm in the book," Feehan said, then hung up.

Florey slammed down the instrument. Feehan was such an ass he could probably pass off a few pages of his own as Frank O'Rourke's unfinished novel. He actually put a piece of paper in Mrs. Ordway's typewriter and stared at the blank expanse for ten minutes. As he sat there, he shuffled remembered openings of O'Rourke stories and novels in his mind, seeking the typical note, but there was none, not really. That should have lifted all constraints, but suddenly the thought of constructing an ordinary English sentence seemed insurmountably difficult, a task of Herculean proportions. He recalled his inner mockery of Agnes's ambition. How amusing. Now he realized that his attitude toward her efforts had contained the assumption that he himself could write if he cared to. Agnes might find it hard, she might produce wretched prose, but if Bill Florey ever chose to put pen to paper, or fingertips to typewriter keys, watch out. He turned off the machine when he realized he was in imminent danger of calling all good men to the aid of their party. Ye gods.

He would have to go back to the Mackin house. As he

had done earlier that evening, he could call and tell Phyllis he was coming out. She had left him alone in the den while he searched for those pages she had identified as Frank's work-in-progress, an unfinished novel. It was not in the four-drawer file cabinet that contained the O'Rourke papers. The top drawer contained unpublished pieces, the others were jammed with the many drafts and versions the author had made of work eventually published. Frank O'Rourke had thrown nothing away—except wives and children.

Phyllis came into the den as he was carefully going through the top drawer for the third time. She clung to his arm.

"Let's go sit by the pool. This house is so stuffy."

Her breath was boozy and the robe she wore was not tightly tied. The sight of her body invited an involuntary comparison with Agnes. Feehan's threat had caused him to see Phyllis with different eyes, unflattering eyes. She was a woman in middle age, flabby, drunk. It would be said he had taken advantage of her. Well, he had. It had seemed extra insurance, as if he were in danger of being shipped back east. He had told Phyllis he loved the Middle West.

"Well," she said in her earthy way, "you've certainly been putting down roots."

Her tug on his arm as he stood at the filing cabinet disgusted him, but he bent and kissed her cheek. They might have been a married couple.

"What are you looking for, Bill?"

"Nothing in particular."

He did not dare ask about the unfinished novel, still hoping he would find it without her help, or knowing. He had learned that Phyllis was never so drunk that she forgot what he said to her. If he mentioned her brother's work-in-progress and afterward it was missing, she would remember. But it was already missing. Somehow it must have been put into one of the other cabinet drawers. The thought of going through them all, with the deadline of Feehan's phone call pressing on him, made Bill Florey jumpy. And Phyllis would not let go.

"Come on," she urged, tugging him from the den. "Let's sit by the pool."

Her girlish manner only made her seem more pathetic. The robe fell open and she did not seem to notice or care. So they had gone out and sat by the pool while the time for Feehan's phone call drew nearer and nearer. Finally, Florey had bolted and driven in a panic to his office, getting there just in time for Feehan's threatened phone call.

He decided that if he went back to the house again, this time he would go unannounced. The difficulty with that was the hours they kept there. Phyllis could put off retiring endlessly and Kevin was more than glad to keep her company. Even without company, Phyllis stayed up until one or two in the morning.

It was all to the better for what he must do that he go to the house late. It was after one o'clock in the morning when he walked up the familiar driveway to the house. As often as he had been there before, he felt like an intruder. His effort to walk soundlessly made him feel like the thief he suddenly realized he was.

The following morning, his primary concern was that no one learn he had been at the Mackin house on Tuesday night, but of course Feehan knew. When he called Feehan in the morning, the news of Phyllis Mackin's death was not yet a public matter, but the police had contacted Bill Florey by telephone.

"Did you get it?" Feehan asked, but his voice quavered.

"You can pick it up at my office. I'll leave it with my secretary."

"No. Bring it to me."

"It will be in an envelope addressed to you."

Florey hung up.

Should he even turn the pages over to Feehan, now that Phyllis was dead? He had weighed the matter carefully. Either way was risky, but not giving Feehan the O'Rourke short story, billed as the beginning of a novel, seemed the riskier. If Feehan required provocation in order to remember that Bill Florey had been to the Mackin house on Tuesday, not giving him the O'Rourke manuscript would have sufficed. Florey had thought of denying he had gone back to the house, but Feehan could still say he had agreed to do so, and that would be just as damaging.

No matter how he looked at it, he was in Feehan's hands now, far more than he had been when the librarian came to his office. It was useless to wish now that he had simply thrown him out and defied him to tell Agnes and the world. It was pointless to wonder just how Feehan would have gone about telling people he was having an affair with Phyllis. How would he have told Agnes? It did not matter. Whatever might have been, he now was where he now was.

He only hoped he was right in thinking Feehan would not know an incomplete short story from the start of a novel.

22

TUTTLE had not expected Jim Feehan to fall for the old selective-theft-from-the-safe story and he had prepared several lines of retreat when the librarian threatened to raise hell if Tuttle did not produce his letters pronto.

That Peanuts had believed the letters were stolen proved nothing. Delphine just snapped her gum and nodded when he called her into his office, pointed to his open safe, and told her he had been robbed. She picked up the phone and handed it to him.

"What's that for?"

"I don't know the emergency number to call the police."

He took the receiver from her and replaced it. "There is no hurry about informing the police. What you might do is get hold of Mr. James Feehan. Close my door, too."

Did Delphine listen in on his conversations? He supposed she did. Even if she did not do it deliberately, she could have overheard almost everything through the thin walls of his suite. He didn't care. In fact, he sort of liked the idea of having an audience to play to while he dealt with clients.

Feehan was not a typical client. Most of Tuttle's clients were in deep trouble with the law and were accordingly meek and docile. After the staged robbery of the safe, Tuttle began to suspect that Feehan was not so untypical after all.

Feehan had come to the office when summoned and he had accepted the story of the theft. Most revealing of all, he had agreed the police should not be informed. He even sat still for the suggestion that Peanuts should tail him to see if he had been followed. Of course it helped that Feehan was sure he knew who the thief was. Paul Gardiner. So Tuttle told Peanuts he really meant it: keep an eye on Feehan. There was no need to tell Peanuts that it was all right if Feehan was aware of his surveillance. It was hard to imagine anyone not being aware of Peanuts following him. Meanwhile, Tuttle would find out what he could about Paul Gardiner.

If Feehan thought Gardiner would break into a practically impregnable safe for those letters, Gardiner should be willing to pay a fair price for them.

Unethical? The thought simply did not occur to Tuttle. Anyone who came to him for legal advice became a client, and a client, in Tuttle's world, was someone from whom to extract as much money as possible. When Feehan had handed over those letters to Tuttle, he had provided the little lawyer with a problem: how best use the letters for maximum results? The solution was obvious. Paul Gardiner. The further difficulty this suggested, finding the young man, resolved itself when Gardiner got in touch with Tuttle.

"I have something you want," Tuttle said.

☆ 155 ☆

"Letters."

Gardiner was a treat to deal with. A point of assignation was agreed upon. Tuttle arrived five minutes early. Gardiner came five minutes late. Taking the letters from Tuttle, he examined them with care.

"Feehan gave you these?"

"That's right."

Gardiner began to laugh. Tuttle became uneasy. He suggested that Gardiner hand over the money. It had been his plan to whet Gardiner's appetite with half the letters, up the ante, and offer him the remainder. Now, given the young man's hilarious response, he doubted he would get the agreed-upon sum. He was right.

"They're forgeries, Tuttle. Utterly worthless."

"Give them to me."

But Gardiner chose not to do so. He put them in his pocket. "Maybe not utterly worthless."

Tuttle's major regret was that he had not brought Peanuts along. By himself, he was no match for Paul Gardiner. So the man walked off and was gone and the problem of finding him presented itself anew.

Paul Gardiner had gone through Fox River like Hansel and Gretel, scattering a trail so obvious Tuttle became cautious. He thought it was dumb luck when it turned out that Paul Gardiner had stayed at the first motel he called, but twelve calls later he hit another. He had moved on, but if his motive was to throw off possible pursuers, he needed expert advice. Even an amateur would have registered under different names. It wasn't enough simply to change motels every once in a while. The thing that bothered him was that Gardiner had not been very fussy about where he stayed—not the mark of a man with lots of money.

If it was easy to learn where Paul Gardiner had been in Fox River, it was not easy to find where he was now. Tuttle was reduced to searching for a pattern in the motels in which Gardiner had stayed, but for the life of him he could not see one. Where the hell had the guy gone?

When Jane Sisson called him from the *Messenger*, Tuttle was more irritated than anything. At first.

"I got something maybe good, Tuttle."

"So what is it?"

He had represented Jane's younger brother on a car-theft charge and she had given him credit for the judge's leniency. But Mullins let off all first offenders. Not that he had told Jane and her brother that. On the contrary, he had filled them with stories of Mullins as a hanging judge and that had made the love feast of the courtroom appearance all the sweeter. Jane had pledged eternal gratitude.

"I don't know if you can use it, but . . ."

"I'll be the judge of that, Jane."

He listened, standing beside his desk with his hat on. Movie-star gossip, for God's sake. Was Jane dumber than he thought? She worked the switchboard at the *Messenger* and Tuttle regarded her as his private early edition. Between her and Peanuts, he was as well-informed a lawyer as Fox River could boast, not that anyone had ever boasted of Tuttle.

"What's the name of the actress?" Tuttle yawned.

"Greta Vanden. You don't see much of her anymore."

"Sure I do. I like late TV."

"Anyway, her son's been in town and Flo Eberle is onto it. I mean, long-distance calls to California, the whole thing."

"What's he doing in Fox River?"

"You tell me. His name is Paul Gardiner."

Tuttle nearly fell over the desk getting into his chair. This information suggested that Gardiner was indeed a worthy object of pursuit. The son of a movie actress ought to be able to pay plenty for Feehan's letters. He had said they were not entirely worthless. They had meant enough to him so that he snatched them from Tuttle's hand. But letters or whatever, there had to be some lever with which to pry money from a man whose mother had made millions. For Tuttle, it was axiomatic that movie stars were millionaires.

"What was the phone number in California, Jane?"

He jotted it down. "I wonder when he left Fox River?"

"Did he leave?"

"Didn't he?"

"I don't know. Say, did you already know about this, Tuttle?"

"Not the details, Jane. I owe you. Keep in touch."

"Forget it," Jane said in a husky voice. "I owe you."

She hung up. Apparently her kid brother was keeping his nose clean. Tuttle feared that any relapse on the brother's part might be blamed on him. He put his feet on his desk and tipped his hat over his eyes. The Irish tweed was his thinking cap. That's why he wore it all year round. A sweaty head was a small price to pay.

Some minutes later he instructed Delphine to put through a call to the California number.

There was no answer.

Tuttle decided that Paul Gardiner was still in Fox River and, if he was, he meant to find him.

But it was Peanuts who found him. Gardiner had come to see Feehan. And Peanuts, not having received contrary instructions, was still tailing the librarian.

23

FLOREY'S secretary handed over the envelope without meeting his eye and for a moment Jim Feehan felt the apprentice felon's desire to do the foul deed and be applauded for it. Or at least to be forgiven. Maybe just understood.

"I hope I didn't get you in trouble with your boss, bursting in on him the other day."

Mrs. Ordway paused momentarily in her typing. Her matronly air was somewhat compromised by the orange nail polish she seemed to be holding out to dry as her hands hung over the keyboard.

"Mr. Florey left that envelope for you. He said to give it to you. Period."

Her hands descended on the keys as if to punctuate the remark.

Feehan shrugged, smiled complicitously to an imaginary audience, turned, and left, the envelope under his arm. Now that he had it, he felt a strange mixture of emotions: elation, power, depression. In this envelope was Frank O'Rourke's unfinished novel. He pressed the envelope against his side, surprised at how small a package it was. But what an impact it would have! How painful to acknowledge that he himself would play only an unsung role in bringing this precious document to the public. He would have to hand it over to Paul Gardiner in exchange for a bundle of phony letters. The descent in the elevator seemed a symbol of his present plight.

When he got back to his office in the library, he felt that Miss Potter provided a pleasant contrast to Mrs. Ordway. His secretary's smile was toothy, her complexion peaches and cream, the blond hair that concealed an absence of brains silky, but Feehan was in no mood to enjoy any of this. Though what enjoying Miss Potter amounted to, even in the best of times, was a source of further depression.

"I will take a call from Paul Gardiner and from no one else."

"Paul Gardiner." She wrote it down. "Mr. Huebner in Circulation asked to see you. The girls at the desk are complaining about a man who has been sitting around the reading room for days."

"What's wrong with that?"

"He isn't reading."

"Is he doing anything else?"

"You mean . . ." Her eyes widened, azure orbs in glistening whites.

"Yes."

"They didn't say."

"They would have said. I can't be bothered with it. Let Huebner handle it. Better yet, let him forget it. This is a public library, after all."

He went into his office, closed the door, sat at his desk, lit a cigarette, and waited. If Gardiner granted him the full forty-eight hours, he had a long wait ahead of him. Was it perhaps Gardiner the girls in Circulation were complaining about? Hope rose but quickly died. No. The girls would not complain if Paul Gardiner sat in the reading room not reading.

Suddenly the more than half century he had spent inhaling and exhaling on planet earth weighed on Feehan's shoulders like a physical object. Why hadn't he married and had children to serve as outward signs of his advancing age? He still thought of himself as a young man. In his mind, he and Paul Gardiner were contemporaries. How absurd that was. How absurd that at his age he should still be lusting after the likes of Miss Potter and bedding dissatisfied housewives like Doris and Agnes. To call these two women housewives had the ring of an insult, given their inflated and groundless hopes, but, even more, it stung Jim Feehan's self-esteem. My God, he was a contemporary of Frank O'Rourke. They had been boys together. Frank O'Rourke, the writer Agnes and Doris thought of as a legendary figure out of the past. He was as distant in their image of time as Henry James was in Feehan's. Well, maybe Fitzgerald, but the point was clear. He was far too old to be catting around the way he did. Thanks to a healthy prostate, good metabolism and . . .

Feehan rose and opened the closet door to examine himself in the mirror attached to its inner side. Good-looking? What did that mean? His eyes were his best feature and his expression was one that conveyed quizzical good humor, as if the world, or the person before him, both surprised and charmed him. It was an expression that conferred importance on its object. Jim Feehan was one of those prone to say he was interested in people. And so he was, as instruments of his own wishes and desires. But most of those who came within range of his intriguing gaze were out to make use of him. Like Paul Gardiner.

Scowling, Feehan returned to his desk. He looked at his watch. He lit another cigarette and tried not to think of the sherry in the cabinet under the window.

The intercom squawked and Miss Potter's voice announced that Mr. Gardiner had arrived.

"Send him in."

The door of the office opened as Feehan was giving these instructions. Paul Gardiner, his brows raised invitingly, his mouth a straight line, came across the room to Feehan's desk.

"Where is it?"

"Did you bring the letters?"

"*Quid pro quo*, Feehan. Where is it?"

Feehan had put the envelope in his "out" tray, thinking that as good a hiding place as any. Apparently Gardiner's eye was caught by Florey's return address in the corner of the envelope. Perhaps, against his will, unwittingly, Feehan had glanced at the tray and drawn Gardiner's attention to it. In any case, Gardiner reached for the envelope, bringing Feehan to his feet, scrambling to snatch back what he had extorted from Florey.

"So this is it."

"Where are my letters?"

"You do well to call them yours, Feehan. But what earthly good are they, to you or anyone else? We agree they are fakes. Make yourself some others if you want."

"You bastard, I want the letters you stole."

Gardiner, grinning and on his way to the door, stopped and looked back at Feehan, somewhat as a maiden aunt might look at a wayward nephew. He came slowly back to Feehan's desk.

"How did you get hold of this, by the way?" A thought

seemed to cross his mind, clouding his face. He opened the envelope and drew forth the sheets. After a moment he nodded and returned them to the envelope. "Well?"

"I didn't steal it, the way you stole my letters."

"Just asked for it, did you?"

"As a matter of fact, yes."

"And she said, by all means, here it is."

"I dealt with her agent. Her lawyer. What difference does it make? Gardiner, I want my letters back."

"Of course you do. And I'll tell you why. Once they are back in your hands, you will be free to say where this is." He flourished the Manila envelope. "Not a chance, Feehan. Those letters are my insurance."

Feehan had been on his feet. Now he sat down so swiftly the chair seemed to rise to meet him. "You don't need any insurance," he said weakly.

"I'll be the judge of that." He paused; when he continued, his tone had altered, dropping many degrees. "Your career as the bosom companion of Frank O'Rourke's youth is over, Feehan. The vultures are being scattered."

Feehan stared at the closed door after Gardiner had gone. The intercom buzzed but he ignored it. A minute later there was a timid tapping on the door. It opened and Miss Potter looked in.

"He's gone."

"Gardiner? Of course he's gone."

"I mean the man in the reading room."

Feehan had no reply to this inanity.

"Did you hear the news of the woman who drowned? Mrs. Markey? No, Mackey. No . . ."

"Mackin!" he roared.

"Yes, that's it. She was found this morning in a pool . . ."

Jim Feehan leaped to his feet and headed for the door, bound he knew not where. Away from his office and its reminder of humiliation, away from Miss Potter and her empty-headed suggestion that life went on as before with the usual quota of disasters. Mrs. Mackin. Phyllis.

He decided he was on his way to the *Messenger*. What better place to wallow in that trivialization of life called news?

24

PHIL KEEGAN'S ear was not particularly sensitive, but he could not ignore the regional accent in Bill Florey's voice with its suggestion of the wisdom of the East. Florey had said several times how much he liked Illinois in general and Fox River in particular, and there was no reason to doubt him—he had certainly been doing well with Finn, Fleischer and Fish; "Fish, Fleischer, Finn and Florey," the lawyer corrected with a tight smile—but that New York accent made it all sound somehow condescending to Phil Keegan.

Besides, he was having trouble understanding just exactly what Florey had done for Phyllis. Of course he was influenced by the phone call too.

"You took care of her legal business?"

Florey considered the back of his right hand. He wore an onyx ring and might have been consulting its opaque surface. "Any lawyer could have done that."

"You were more than a lawyer?"

"I represented her interests in the matter of her brother's literary estate," Florey said primly. "The rights to the stories and novels of Frank O'Rourke are immensely valuable just now. Some of us consider this to be merely the beginning and predict that O'Rourke will occupy a permanent position in American literature. But right now there is a good deal of money to be made from his literary properties. Reprints, movie and television adaptations, the lot. My experience in Manhattan enabled me to act as Mrs. Mackin's representative and to assure that she received just compensation."

"You've been doing pretty well for her?"

"It can be said that Mrs. Mackin was doing very well, yes." Reference to Phyllis enabled him to frown away the implied compliment in the question.

"How well is well?"

"Do you want figures, details?" Florey seemed genuinely surprised.

"Yes. Could you make that information available to us?"

"I could, yes. But I wonder if I should."

"You should. Mr. Florey, we have a murder case here. At least that is what the prosecutor has decided and that makes your records on the business dealings of the deceased relevant."

"Relevant to motive?"

"We can of course subpoena the stuff."

Florey showed the palm of his hand, tipped his head, smiled. "You can have them, Captain. No problem. Believe me, on this investigation you can count on my total cooperation. You did say murder?"

"Homicide to some degree, anyway. No accident. We've ruled that out."

"She was a great lady, Captain."

"Tell me about her."

Listening to Florey, Keegan was barely able to discover some glimpses of Phyllis behind the laudatory account the lawyer gave. Phyllis was a great lady—just what one would expect of the sister of an author as perceptive and insightful as Frank O'Rourke. It had been a high point of Florey's career when he was asked to represent Mrs. Mackin, and whatever money he had managed to amass for her over the years was small enough return for the privilege. He had been honored to know her.

"Didn't she drink?"

"You mean to excess?"

"I mean all the time."

Florey thought about this with a little frown. "I wouldn't judge her in the way your remark seems to, Captain. She drank, yes. She had a problem there, but it was a problem under control."

"You never saw her drunk?"

"No, I'd say not. Of course, when I would see her . . ."

"How often did you see her?"

"It varied, depending on what negotiations were in progress. I kept her informed on everything, of course. I saw her a lot."

"We received a phone call suggesting that you were having an affair with Mrs. Mackin."

"Did he lisp?" Florey had not turned a hair.

"Why do you ask that?"

"Because your caller was most likely Kevin, the man, more or less, who cooked for Mrs. Mackin."

Keegan picked up his phone and asked to be put through to Horvath. "Cy, come in here, will you?"

While they waited for Horvath to come in, Keegan said nothing. Florey seemed completely unflustered by the charge— with all its enormous implications—that he had been having an affair with Phyllis Mackin. When Horvath came in, he remained standing.

"Cy, about that anonymous call we had about Mr. Florey and Mrs. Mackin. Did the caller lisp?"

Cy thought about it, then shook his head. "No."

"Did he sound in any way effeminate?" Florey asked.

Keegan said, "Mr. Florey thinks it might have been Kevin, the guy who . . ."

Horvath shook his head. "No, I talked with him at the house. I'd know the voice. It wasn't Kevin."

"Why did you think Kevin would call up here and say a thing like that?" Keegan asked Florey, at the same time waving Cy to a chair. He wanted Cy in on this. The longer he talked to Florey, the less he liked him. Even so, the idea of this guy having anything going with Phyllis seemed ridiculous. But Keegan felt the lawyer's reactions did not ring true.

"Kevin was very possessive about Mrs. Mackin. He resented the fact that I had immediate access to her. Often I needed swift authorizations. Once I came before she was out of bed and Kevin made rather a point of the fact that I had seen her in her bedroom."

"Couldn't you have gotten authorizations on the phone?"

"Not when a signature was needed."

"When did you last see Mrs. Mackin?"

"I've already told you that. On Tuesday."

"The day she died."

"Yes. I saw her the evening of the day before she was found in the pool."

"You got that information, Cy?"

Horvath closed his eyes, then opened them. "He arrived at maybe seven-thirty and left before nine."

"At eight forty-five, if you want to be exact. Phyllis Mackin was alive and well when I left her house."

"Who else was there at the time?"

"In the house? Kevin, I imagine."

"And Mr. Mackin."

"Oh, of course. Obviously he was always there."

"You don't like Kevin, do you?"

"I don't like the type, Captain. I never have."

"Do you think there was something going on between him and Mrs. Mackin?"

Florey's laugh was a little bark. "Apparently you don't understand what I mean by Kevin's type."

"You mean he's queer?"

"He does nothing to conceal it."

Horvath said, "It wasn't Kevin who phoned."

"Do you have any other ideas who might call and say a thing like that, Mr. Florey?"

"No. And I don't see that it matters. The story is manifestly foolish and false. I acted as Mrs. Mackin's lawyer and nothing else."

"But you liked her a lot?"

"I admired her immensely. Captain, I don't know how old I look to you . . ."

"How old are you?"

"I'm forty-two. Phyllis Mackin was in her fifties."

"I wish I knew who made that call," Keegan said.

"Why?"

"Because whoever did must be trying to divert attention to you. And away from himself. If we knew . . ."

"I see what you mean." Florey liked the idea. He wanted the subject changed, or at least the direction in which the conversation seemed to be going. The thought of himself as object of someone's vindictive gossip was welcome.

"Well, let's get back to Mrs. Mackin."

"Captain, do you know a man named James Feehan?"

Keegan, who had been fishing for a cigarette, left his

hand inside his suit jacket. After a split second he withdrew it and Florey's eyes were on the cigarette as if the detective had just produced a rabbit. His eyes lifted to Keegan's.

"Yes, Mr. Florey, I know Feehan."

"He could have been the one who phoned here."

"Why do you say that?"

"Because he came to me a few days ago with the same story, threatening to tell my wife about it. That's why I wasn't surprised to hear you mention it. Isn't it weird how the craziest story gains plausibility simply by being spoken aloud and repeated?"

"What day was that?"

"That Feehan threatened me?" Florey consulted his memory. "Monday. Maybe Tuesday."

The words "will be my good news day" formed in Keegan's mind, distracting him with their vague suggestion of other and better times. His wife had sung that song.

"Tuesday was the day you visited Mrs. Mackin," Horvath said.

"I had an appointment with her that day, yes."

"The day Feehan came to your home and . . ."

"He came to my office."

"To your office. Good. He came there and said you were carrying on with Mrs. Mackin and he was going to tell your wife about it?"

"That's right." Florey followed Keegan's words as if he now wished he had not mentioned Feehan.

"What did he want?"

"I don't understand."

"What you are describing sounds like blackmail."

"Does it? What he wanted was for me to stop this alleged affair. Perhaps he himself had designs on Mrs. Mackin. They were closer in age, certainly."

"Did he say that?"

"I am inferring, of course. At the time, I simply assumed that's what it was. The poor fellow, if he thought only an imaginary rival stood between him and Phyllis Mackin he was very much mistaken. She despised him."

"She discussed him with you?"

"He claimed to have been a good friend of her brother, the writer. This was false. She despised him for trying to exploit a relationship that never existed. Seems to have been a habit of his."

"How so?" Keegan asked.

"My alleged affair with Mrs. Mackin. He made that up too."

"If he was the one who telephoned," Horvath said.

"That he called you is an assumption on my part, but, as you can see, not without foundation. What did the caller sound like?"

"Just a male voice."

"Did it sound like Feehan, Cy?"

"All I'm sure of is that it wasn't Kevin."

"Captain, I can understand how helpful it would be to find out who called here, but I can't really help you."

"Maybe you have."

"That would please me, needless to say. I hope you will treat my guesses as confidential."

"How did your wife react?"

"Good God, you don't imagine I carried that crazy story home to my wife, do you?"

"Why not, if it was false?"

"Are you married, Captain?"

Keegan resented this implicit appeal to expert status. "Your wife wouldn't have liked it?"

"Nobody's wife would like to hear such a preposterous

thing or think her husband was suspected of infidelity, even by a diseased mind like Feehan's. I most certainly did not tell her."

They went back to Mrs. Mackin then, as Florey had suggested they do, and went over the ground Cy had covered on his first interview with the lawyer, a fact Florey mentioned with frequent glances at his watch. Finally Keegan let him go.

"For now," he added.

Florey shot a glance at him. "I said I would help all I can, Captain. But I also have a career."

"I know. I'll try to keep it to a minimum."

"That's funny," Horvath said after Florey was gone.

"What is?"

"His not telling his wife about Mrs. Mackin."

"Oh, I don't know. If it's false, why bring it home? And, if it's true . . ."

"I don't mean that. But she's been shacking up with Feehan."

"Mrs. Florey has?"

"That's right. His secretary told me. Gloria Potter. Feehan is a real busy guy in that department."

"Did you check out the secretary's story?"

"Phil, I've got a list of Feehan's girl friends."

"Don't tell me Mrs. Mackin's on it."

"No, she's not one of them."

Keegan stood.

"Come on, Cy. Let's go talk to Mrs. Florey."

25

W‌HEN the police came, Agnes Florey was half expecting them. Ever since she heard of the death of Phyllis Mackin and increasingly as the details emerged, she had been having the most awful thoughts, unbelievable thoughts, thoughts she did not for a minute take seriously.

Doris Hagstrom said, "Dammit, Agnes, there goes our chance to interview her."

"Doris!"

"I'm just being professional. How can we write a book about Frank O'Rourke now?"

"How can you even think of it? A woman is dead. She was found in the very pool we saw the day we were there. Think about it."

Doris thought about it. She thought maybe they should change the subject of the book. It should concern the murder of Phyllis O'Rourke Mackin.

"Maybe she wasn't even murdered."

Doris half turned her head and regarded Agnes from the corner of her eye. "It's murder. You can bet on it."

Agnes could have clawed out her best friend's eyes for this sassy approach to the death of a human being. Doris seemed to sense the reaction.

"I guess I'm forgetting that Bill has lost a client."

"You have such a delicate way of putting things, Doris."

"When did Bill last see her?"

"Why? What difference does it make?"

"Well, have you ever known someone who was murdered? I never have. If I did, I'd be thinking of the last time I saw them, maybe what they said. You know. Did they perhaps and without knowing they were doing it give some clue as to what was coming? A premonition? I remember the last time I saw my grandmother. She wasn't murdered, she died a natural death, but the last time I talked with her . . ."

Agnes tuned it out. She had come to Doris in search of consolation, but there was no way she could bring up what was really bothering her.

"Well, she was more than just a client to Bill."

"That's isn't true!"

"Of course it's true."

"Doris, there was nothing to it."

Doris shrugged and rolled her eyes. "It's a good thing for you if it isn't true."

"What do you mean?"

"Well, just think of the motive it would give you for conking her over the head and dumping her into the pool. Jealous wife avenges herself."

"That's the silliest thing I ever heard of." Agnes was fuming now and Doris's knowing expression was suddenly more than she could stand. "It's as silly as the thought of your going to bed with Jim Feehan."

"What is that supposed to mean, Agnes?"

"It is supposed to mean that the thought of Bill having an affair with Mrs. Mackin is exactly as silly as the thought of your getting into bed with Jim Feehan."

The air was electric. The two women stared at each other and, though nothing further was said, it was clear to them both that they were no longer best friends. They might not even be friends at all.

It was only when she was back in her own house that Agnes realized she had in effect admitted to Doris that Bill had been sleeping with Phyllis Mackin, because Doris had had something going with Jim Feehan.

So, though Agnes had not gotten to discuss with Doris her fears concerning Bill's absence from the house the night Phyllis Mackin was killed, she was really not surprised when the police came to talk to her. Well, not police exactly. Detectives.

"I am Captain Keegan and this is Lieutenant Horvath."

The conversation with Doris turned out to be an ideal preparation for the interview with Captain Keegan and Lieutenant Horvath. The two of them were nice as could be, taking turns asking questions, and they tried to make them seem like anything but questions. Not that they made any bones about the fact that they had come to talk about Mrs. Mackin, and her husband had been, as they said, lawyer for the deceased.

"You really should talk to Bill."

"We have, Mrs. Florey."

"Well, I can't tell you anything he didn't. I only saw Mrs. Mackin once in my life, to talk to, and then neither of us said anything."

"She must have been an unhappy woman," Lieutenant Horvath said in a sad voice.

"I wouldn't know."

"I meant her husband. You know his condition?"

"Yes. I see what you mean."

"How did they get along?"

"I haven't the least idea."

They talked of marriages then, happy marriages, unhappy marriages, and before she knew it, Agnes no longer felt wary. The two detectives seemed just like anyone else and they were so easy to talk to. That was why, when Captain Keegan asked the question, it came as such a surprise. She just stared at him. He repeated it.

"Do *I* have a happy marriage? What does that have to do with anything?"

The two men fell silent. She looked from one to the other—Lieutenant Horvath looked suddenly silly, a big hulk of a man in a chintz chair; Captain Keegan, chin thrust forward, hands between his knees, his expression inviting her to continue the conversation on the confiding note they had so carefully struck.

"Really, that's insulting."

Agnes stood up but the two men remained seated. Her mind was awhir with the thoughts with which earlier she had gone to Doris. They knew about Bill. They knew about his affair with Mrs. Mackin, and they knew he had been out, somewhere, on the night Mrs. Mackin was killed.

For she had been killed. Murdered. The detectives had been insistent on that. Mrs. Mackin had been struck on the head and was most likely unconscious when she entered the pool. They did not say she was thrown in, but Agnes's mind filled with a shadowy scene. A figure, staggering with its burden, approaching the pool. He straightens up as he flings the body into the water. A tremendous splash, the man turns and it is . . .

"James Feehan," Horvath said. "Do you know him?"

"Feehan!"

"He is head librarian at the Pawnee branch. Also, he edits the Sunday book page of the *Fox River Messenger*. You do know him, don't you?"

"I know who he is, yes." This radical shift in the conversation bewildered Agnes. She sat down again. "I see him at the library."

"Yes," Horvath said.

"He is a friend of yours?" Keegan said.

"What are you getting at?"

"I think you know, Mrs. Florey."

Could they really be interested in her? Could they possibly, even remotely, think . . .

"Did you resent Mrs. Mackin?" Horvath asked.

"The yardman at the Mackin house says you visited there a short time ago, asking lots of questions."

Agnes's laughter sounded hysterical even to herself. "I was there to interview her!"

The two men exchanged glances.

"We were going to write a book, about Frank O'Rourke. *Frank O'Rourke and Fox River*." She traced the words in air before her face, skywriting, spelling out the title of the abortive book she and Doris had meant to write.

"Did you interview Mrs. Mackin?"

"No."

She explained to them the conversation with Hermie. They did not seem to believe her. She invoked Doris and they were unimpressed. But she didn't want them talking to Doris. Thank God, she remembered the tape then. She jumped to her feet and went into Bill's study to get it. When she turned from the desk, holding the cassette, triumphant, Lieutenant Horvath stood watching her from the doorway. Had he thought she was making a break for it?

"I'll play it for you."

"Could we take it with us?"

She considered that. It seemed a way to get them going, so she agreed, but they were not yet finished with her. They wanted to ask about Bill. When had he last seen Mrs. Mackin? She supposed they were checking with her what Bill had already told them and she did not know what he had told them.

"You haven't any idea when your husband last saw Mrs. Mackin?"

"Ask him, for heaven's sake."

"Could it have been last Tuesday?"

"It could have been, yes. How would I know?"

"In the evening? Was your husband home last Tuesday evening?"

"I don't remember."

"Try."

Horvath said, "Your husband says he went to see Mrs. Mackin on Tuesday evening."

"Then why on earth . . ."

"He says that you did not accompany him."

Did that mean Bill *had* said she was with him? She refused to play the game any longer.

"I think I should telephone Bill and have him come here. I don't care to answer any more of your questions."

That ended it. They rose without demur. She stood in the window and watched them go out to their car. She regretted now having given them the cassette. Why should she be of help to people like that?

But of whom were they suspicious, Bill or herself?

26

"IT COULD be either, Roger."

"Or neither. What is the motive?"

"Motive?" Keegan smiled painfully. "Take your choice. Jealousy, revenge, who knows? I guess greed."

"What's missing?"

"The manuscript of the unfinished novel."

"You're sure there was one?"

"Phyllis had announced there was. Florey, the guy who handled all that stuff, agrees. He also says it's missing."

"You think Florey stole it?"

"Why not? This is the man who had complete control of Frank O'Rourke's stuff, he set up all the deals. What did Phyllis know? I'm told that unfinished novel is worth plenty."

"It can't be published, can it? Any publisher who brought it out would be sued."

"By whom?"

Roger Dowling thought about that. He did not want to mention Paul Gardiner, unsure whether Phil had yet identified the man as the son of Frank O'Rourke. Even without that identification, he was a primary object of concern in the investigation. And he had not yet been located.

"We don't even know if Gardiner was in town last Tuesday," Keegan had said earlier, and Roger Dowling knew this was only a feeble effort to ease the pain.

They should have located Paul Gardiner long ago, certainly Phil Keegan would think so. But people who are objects of nationwide police searches elude their pursuers for years. Sometimes forever. If nothing else, Keegan would want to hear from Gardiner himself that he had not been in town Tuesday, with proof of the fact. But whatever a tracked-down Gardiner might say, Roger Dowling knew he could not prove he was out of Fox River last Tuesday. Almost certainly he had been in town. Marie Murkin had seen him.

"When I asked about his fiancée, he just stared at me. You would have thought he had never seen me before."

"Where was this, Marie?"

She had come upon Gardiner when she was looking for her car in the vast lot of a new shopping center just southwest of Fox River. Roger Dowling did not approve of the housekeeper buying groceries in such places. Shops in the immediate neighborhood needed all the patronage they could get, no matter that Mrs. Murkin complained of the prices in the grocery two blocks away. It was his theory that by walking and saving gas she would actually be paying less.

"Did he have a car?"

"I suppose. What else would he be doing in a parking lot?"

"He probably didn't recognize you."

"I told you he didn't."

"You know how it is when you see people out of context, out of their usual setting."

Mrs. Murkin didn't like that. "Are you saying I'm some kind of church mouse?"

"It's better than being a shopping-mall mouse."

He drove to the mall himself some hours later, an irrational sort of thing to do, but after all the place was where Paul Gardiner had last been seen, at least as far as Roger Dowling knew. He strolled through the vast air-conditioned expanse of the shopping mall, past boutique after boutique, all of them looking very much alike. There was a fountain, of course. There was always a fountain in such places. It was a wonder the water didn't freeze, they kept the place so cold.

When he went outside again, the temperature seemed by contrast equatorial. He felt a sudden lethargy, but the heat was welcome too. He sat for a moment in his car, enjoying a heat that would shortly be intolerable. It was when he was leaving the parking lot that he noticed the motel.

That was what it was called. Motel. It was low and long, stucco, and a row of wilting hollyhocks planted along the wall seemed an ineffectual effort to provide privacy from the busy street, or perhaps they were only meant to conceal the building. Roger Dowling had read somewhere that motels were built to last no more than twenty-five years, and this place, the Motel motel, had certainly long since entered into its obsolescence.

Father Dowling pulled into the drive and came to a stop beneath a sagging overhang. Through the screen door of the office he heard the roar of the television. The man behind the desk, looking through the screen door like a computer-produced picture, one constructed of all Xs, did not turn from the television to see who had stopped at his door. Roger Dowling got out of the car and went inside.

When the man turned he could not conceal his surprise. He addressed Roger Dowling's collar. "Yes sir?"

"How are you?" Roger Dowling said affably, looking around. There wasn't much to see. Two plastic easy chairs, some of their cracks repaired with tape, the reception desk, the television set perched on a ledge almost ceiling high. On a small table a coffee machine bubbled. Roger Dowling wondered if the promise of free breakfast on the sign outside referred to the coffee pot. He asked about the free breakfast.

"You want a room?"

"What do you charge?"

"I don't know if I got anything free."

The man's chest was so broad that Roger Dowling doubted he could cross his arms, but his height robbed that wrestler's expanse of its effect; the clerk could not be much more than five feet tall.

"Do you own this place?"

The man ignored the question. He looked up from a spiral notebook he had been flipping through. "Nope. All units are full. Sorry."

"That's all right."

"You didn't want a room, did you?"

The man looked up at Roger Dowling through very thick lenses, fearful of the answer. Did he think the priest had come to perform some mysterious liturgical deed right before his eyes? Roger Dowling explained he was looking for a man named Paul Gardiner and had reason to believe he might have stayed in this motel.

"I can't give out information like that."

"Good heavens, man, you can see that I'm a priest."

The clerk and perhaps owner as well decided he did not

want to know why a priest would be looking for Paul Gardiner. He went back to his spiral notebook. Paul Gardiner had rented a unit in the Motel motel the previous Monday.

"You mean Monday night?"

"Check-out time is noon. I don't enforce that exactly, but he would have been out by two on Tuesday, that's for sure."

It had been midafternoon when Marie had seen him in the parking lot. Paul Gardiner, when he registered, gave a California address. Roger Dowling wondered as he jotted it down if it was the same one Flo Eberle would not give him. He thanked the clerk.

"You from around here, Reverend?"

"Fox River."

"No wonder you wouldn't want a room. A unit. If I had one free, I mean."

On the screen incredible troubles unraveled in the course of interminable conversations. The clerk's eye was drawn back to the television. Flo Eberle should hire him to do her watching for her.

This was not the first time he had known things Phil Keegan would have liked to know but had not told him, yet Roger Dowling was uncomfortable sitting in Phil's office and talking about the investigation of Mrs. Mackin's murder and not telling Phil that Gardiner was Frank O'Rourke's son and had been in Fox River on the day of the murder. Phil could add to his list of possible motives if he knew those two facts.

"Do you think he went back to California, Phil?"

"They're keeping an eye out for him."

The Fox River search for Paul Gardiner had turned up motels in which Gardiner had stayed, but Phil did not have enough people to speed up the search. Besides, he had other fish to fry. Why assume it was an out-of-towner when Fox River itself had several prime candidates of its own? Roger

Dowling had to remind himself that Phil did not know who Paul Gardiner really was. There was amusement in Phil's voice when he spoke of the book Agnes Florey and Doris Hagstrom had meant to write.

"Did you listen to the cassette?"

Keegan took a player from a drawer of his desk and punched a button. Roger Dowling sat forward at the sound of the male voice.

"Who is that speaking?"

"The yardman. Hermie. They interviewed the yardman," Phil said with an incredulous chuckle.

"Wait, don't turn it off."

Phil paused with his finger over the off key while the voice spoke on and on. He turned it off when Horvath came into the office. The expression on the lieutenant's face was as close as he came to looking excited.

"We've located Paul Gardiner."

Keegan got to his feet. "Good. Who found him?"

"Pianone."

"Peanuts!" Keegan looked as if he meant to sit down again. "Is he sure?" Doubt that Peanuts could successfully identify his own uncle was heavy in Keegan's voice.

"It's Gardiner, all right. Hanson got a glimpse of him before they lost him."

Keegan hit his forehead with the palm of his hand. "That's more like it. That sounds like Peanuts."

Roger Dowling declined the halfhearted invitation that he come along. When Phil and Cy had left, the priest went to the desk and turned on the cassette again, rewinding it so he could hear it all from the beginning. There did not seem to be any doubt whose voice it was.

27

FATHER Dowling turned into the driveway at the Mackin house when he saw the man he had come to talk to bouncing across the lawn at the wheel of a tractor mower. He hoped they wouldn't mind his old car being parked so conspicuously in front of the house, but then, it was difficult to know who "they" might be. Mr. Mackin could scarcely object and the cook's opinion did not matter.

When he got out of the car he deliberately slammed the door, but the noise did not reach Herman. How could it, when he was riding in the roar of the tractor mower, its large half-muffled motor assaulting the summer air. Roger Dowling started across the lawn toward a point at which he would be in the path of the mower.

Even at that it seemed Hermie would not see him and Roger Dowling would have to jump to one side lest he be run over. Hermie was bent over the steering wheel, he wore a plastic baseball helmet and sunglasses. Suddenly his head jerked up and he put on the brakes.

Roger Dowling went around the mower to speak to its driver, looking into a face shaded by the peak of the cap, eyes invisible behind the opaque lenses of the sunglasses. Roger Dowling could not hear his own voice when he spoke.

"What?" Hermie's compensatory shout was all too audible. Roger Dowling stepped back and smiled.

"I want to talk to you." He exaggerated the formation of the words, relying on the man to read his lips rather than hear him.

Hermie reached forward and turned a key. The noise fell away, seeming to return to its source from across the lawn, to descend from the overhanging branches of the trees. How blessedly welcome the silence was.

"I couldn't hear you, Father."

"I said I'd like to talk to you."

The sunglasses came off, leaving pale discs on the tanned face above the beard. "I'm mowing the lawn."

"When will you finish?"

"What is it you want to talk about?"

" 'The gash of the river on the green body of Illinois.' "

The eyes surrounded by the pale untanned skin caused by the wearing of sunglasses were the bluer for it. They studied Father Dowling for perhaps half a minute, then turned to survey the lawn.

"I won't be long. What's your name?"

"Roger Dowling. I'm the pastor of Saint Hilary's parish."

"No kidding!"

"Where should I wait for you?"

"Who's with you?"

"I'm alone."

"That your car in the drive?"

"Yes."

"Take it on down by the garage. I'll be bringing the mower down there when I finish."

"You live over the garage, don't you?"

"You seem to know a lot about me."

"That's true."

At the turn of the key, the awful racket of the motor began again. Roger Dowling was glad to escape from it to his car. He started it and eased the car up toward the pool, took the turn to the left, and a moment later stopped on the apron of the four-car garage. It seemed to date from a time earlier than the house and to suggest a different era of affluence. When he got out of his car, the sound of the mower, tolerable from this distance, came to him, filtered through the intervening trees and shrubs. He strolled up to the pool so he could watch the mower finish the task.

The wheelchair came at him much as the mower had earlier, but this time there was no last-minute reprieve. Roger Dowling got his hands out and grabbed the arms of the onrushing chair, knocking the occupant's hand from the control panel. This cut the power, but Roger Dowling found himself running backward, trying to equalize the movement of the chair. Finally he had to push himself to the side and he fell heavily on the flagstone that encircled the pool. His pushing off had the effect of sending the chair in a great lazy circle.

The heel of one of his hands was scraped and bleeding, his elbow stung with pain, and the fronts of his legs, above his knees, burned from the initial collision. Roger Dowling, seated on the flagstone, watched the invalid, as out of control as his vehicle, head swinging helplessly on his shoulders as if it must soon roll off and go bumping down the incline toward the garage. A strange moaning sound brought Roger Dowling to his feet. He went after the chair, caught and stopped it.

"Are you all right?"

The moaning seemed to alter in pitch.

"That's all right. You're fine. Everything's okay."

Father Dowling took the head in his hands, stopping its mad gyrations. Mackin's tongue emerged from the side of his mouth and his eyes rolled in their sockets, still out of control, no matter that Roger Dowling held the head immobile.

"It's all right," the priest repeated, trying to establish contact with at least one of Mackin's eyes. How could the man get around in this damnable chair if he could not focus his eyes?

Mackin's hand dropped to the control panel at the roar of the approaching mower. Roger Dowling let go of the head and stepped clear as the wheelchair began to move. Watching Mackin maneuver surely around the edge of the pool and then accelerate as he continued to the house, Roger Dowling found it difficult to put together that sure progress and the almost complete lack of self-control on Mackin's part.

Behind him the roar of the tractor reached a maximum and then began to fade as Herman directed it down to the garage. Roger Dowling felt that he was involved in a problem in grade-school mathematics: two vehicles departing from a fixed point in different directions and at different rates of speed, which would arrive in Wichita first? He started down toward the garage.

The tractor had gone out of sight around the garage and its sound was muffled and then abruptly died. After a minute, Herman appeared. He approached Father Dowling with his hands in his pockets. The cap and glasses were gone.

"How did you know, Father?"

"Not by looking at you, certainly."

"No, I daresay not. Age and a grizzled beard work wonders."

"Far more important is the fact that no one would expect to see a dead man."

"Let's go inside. This fresh air is killing me."

And so, with Frank O'Rourke leading the way, the two men went up the narrow stairs to the apartment over the garage.

28

THERE is an age, and it varies with personal imagination, that marks the end of the upward incline of life. Prior to reaching it, hope is an infinitely tappable resource, the evils of the day will soon give way to tomorrow's goods, the flaws in one's character are corrigible, mere temporary residents of the soul, fundamentally unserious. When the crucial age is reached, however, one despairs of being otherwise than one is, tomorrow promises only a repetition of today or worse, the future is seen to be one long declension to the grave.

For Frank O'Rourke, 44 had been the age that seemed the hinge of life. For more than a decade before that fateful birthday, he had been, in the eyes of almost everyone else, on his way to hell in a hand basket. He was a drunk. He was a fugitive, unfaithful husband. As a parent, he was worse than a failure. He had wasted what estimable critics considered to be one of the finest literary talents of his generation.

But during the decade that to others had marked his nadir, he himself continued to believe that on the morrow he could write again at no greater price than sitting down to his typewriter. He was equally certain he could stop drinking. Tomorrow. He firmly believed his next marriage would be his last. Sometimes he even thought he could redeem himself in the eyes of his sons.

The crucial age came and he could no longer resist what had long since been the judgment of others on his life. He tried to stop drinking, and succeeded only in reducing his alcoholic consumption to six bottles of beer a day and he felt like an anchorite in doing so. His former wives would not see him. His sons bore the name of a stranger. His third wife, a nurse, had become addicted to drugs in the line of duty and leaned more and more on him for support. She would have been better advised to lean upon the air. When he sat at his typewriter, the keyboard seemed strange, nothing he had ever confronted before, though he had used it for writing letters long after the flow of fiction from it had ceased. He could not write.

He began to write about a writer who could not write. One day he put a piece of paper in the typewriter and composed a suicide note for his imaginary writer. In the course of doing this, the old power, which is essentially mimickry, returned, but before he reached the end of the page it was gone. All he had managed to do was write the farewell note of a fictive failed novelist. He got up from his desk and poured himself a drink.

It was the first of many. He left his room, his house, and he continued to drink. He drank for days, wandering in strange places only imperfectly seen, blackouts alternating with the return of semiconsciousness and his suicidal thirst. He sobered up in Mexico and had no memory of having gone there. He spent two weeks in the sun, letting the dry heat bake the alcohol from his blood. He felt he had aged twenty years in as many days. His hands retained a tremor that truly frightened him. In the dark, he promised himself or God or both that he would not go on like this. But he was 44 and he did not believe it.

In San Diego he read in a newspaper of his death.

His first reaction was an impulse to laugh. He sought for variations on Mark Twain's remark in a similar situation. But he did not laugh and he lost the desire to refute the claim that he was dead. "I did die," he told himself, "but I am back. I am Lazarus brought back from the grave." It was a second chance. Forty-four had lost its mythic power.

He went back to Illinois, by stages, supporting himself by menial jobs that exhilarated him. In *Travels with Charley*, John Steinbeck wrote of crossing the country in a camper to get back in touch with the wellsprings of America. Compared with Frank O'Rourke's eastward hegira, Steinbeck's travels were safe and insulated. It seemed to O'Rourke that real life, genuine existence, was lived close to the earth, that we need the seasons as a metaphor of the moral life, the great wheel of renewal. It is at our peril that we permit a distance to grow between ourselves and the world on which we depend for survival. He felt a new and better vision grow within him and, as he neared his sister's home and his own native town, he was certain that now he would be able to write again.

Emil Mackin suffered a stroke when he was confronted by his dead brother-in-law. Emil had always been a bit strange, but Frank's homecoming had boosted him into another dimension of oddity.

"How did your sister react?" Father Dowling asked.

"Fortunately, she had the cushion of booze. I was no more real than anything else she was seeing that day. When relative lucidity returned, she was prepared to accept the fact that I was back. And of course Emil's condition distracted her. There was a doubt that he would survive. But he did, though his Easter was less complete than mine."

The priest was not shocked by the remark, as O'Rourke had half expected him to be. How this thin Dantesque priest could be so easy to talk to was difficult to say. Perhaps after all these years of chosen obscurity, he needed to speak. And Phyllis's death seemed to write finis to their long deception.

"The one thing that was not tied up was my literary property. After the second divorce, I had dumped it all on Phyl—copyrights, manuscripts, the lot. Everything else, the insurance, half the profits from my house, had to wait. No corpus delicti, no probate until the fullness of time."

O'Rourke had pressured Phyllis to pressure Fish, Fleischer and Finn to bring in someone with experience in publishing. Florey had done a good job. The great disappointment was that he was unable to do much with the new things Frank O'Rourke wrote in his apartment over the garage. He had never felt more like a writer; he himself liked the stuff he was writing; but Florey could not sell it. Not to editors. Anything done on this typewriter had value with collectors: letters, notes, short stories, the content did not matter. O'Rourkiana.

"You've gone on writing?" Father Dowling asked.

It would have been difficult to deny it, sitting there in the garage apartment. His desk—a flush door supported by trestles—was a bouquet of paper with his typewriter as centerpiece, the same old machine Phyl had managed to get from the flaky Rosita, wife number three, allegedly for sentimental reasons.

"A writer writes," O'Rourke said.

He could see the questions form in the priest's eyes. Would he ask about the unfinished novel he had shown to Phyllis who, damn her, had mentioned it in her cups one day? Work-in-progress. Interrupted not by death but by the depressing realization as he read it over that it was going nowhere. It did not compare with the work that had won him fame and that, more than ever before, was bringing in money, supporting Phyllis and Emil, as well as himself. And paying Kevin's salary. But the priest's question was not about his writing.

"Who killed your sister?"

"The police have been asking me that same question."

"And you've told them you have no idea."

"That's right."

"And not knowing who you really are, they accept that. Why should a yardman who lives over the garage know anything of the real affairs of the house? But you knew a great deal, perhaps everything."

"I have ideas, of course. But the police would want reasons and proof."

"What kind of ideas?"

"Just between us?"

"All right."

"Well, it may sound churlish of me, but consider Bill Florey."

Suddenly it seemed a delicate matter, telling this priest that Phyllis had been carrying on with her lawyer. Of course Emil was useless as a husband. He probably never was much in that department, but you can't expect a priest to see that as an excuse for fooling around.

"What did you think of their affair?"

"I didn't like it. It was unprofessional of him."

"Florey didn't know your true identity, did he?"

"No! Only Phyllis knew. And Emil, if Emil knows anything. So you can see I was in no position to tell Florey to cut it out. What the hell would he care what I think? He guessed my attitude anyway and actually suggested to Phyllis that she get rid of me. The son of a bitch didn't realize I was her bread and butter. And his."

"You think Florey killed your sister?"

"He had the opportunity."

"Because he came to see your sister Tuesday evening? But he left before nine o'clock."

"How do you know that?"

"I have a friend on the police force. Captain Keegan."

"Keegan!"

"That's right, you knew him, didn't you?"

O'Rourke smiled. "Strange how the past tense applies to me, as if I'd never risen from the dead at all. So Keegan confides in you."

"I knew him long ago too."

"Well, he wouldn't have been able to tell you that Florey came back here Tuesday night. He did leave before nine the first time. But he was back here and sitting with Phyllis by the pool long after midnight."

"Why didn't you tell the police that?"

"Are you going to?"

"You asked to speak in confidence."

"And you'd respect that, wouldn't you?" It was a pleasant thought, that he could tell this priest anything with impunity. It would even make going on as before tolerable. In Phyllis he had had a therapeutic listener, someone with whom he could be himself.

"No one has ever suspected you of being Frank O'Rourke?"

"It would have been in the papers if they had. Tell me, how did you find out?"

Frank O'Rourke remembered the two women who had come on their mad errand, hoping to interview Phyllis. He might have suspected, as they sat talking on the bench, that they would have a tape recorder and decide to put it to use, if only to test its efficacy. Why would they want to interview the yardman? But they had wanted his version of a typical day here.

" 'The gash of the river on the green body of Illinois.' Your saying that could merely have been the quoting of the author whose sister was your employer. That alone proved nothing."

"Did I actually say that to those women?"

The priest nodded. "I recognized it from *Where No Storms Come.*"

"And my voice matched that on the cassettes you bought in a bookstore? My voice must be the one thing about me that has not changed."

"To hear it disembodied, on tape, as I did, helps. I doubt that, simply by speaking with you like this, I would have been reminded of the tapes and made the connection."

"Whom have you told?"

"Nobody."

"You mean yet?"

"If you wish to make yourself known, that is up to you."

"Are you suggesting that I do?"

The priest did not answer the question and his expression was unreadable. O'Rourke would have thought Dowling would leap at the chance to give him advice. Wasn't that his job, telling everybody else how to live their lives? He said as much to Dowling, hoping to provoke him into answering his question.

"You sound a good deal like your sister on the subject of religion."

"Poor Phyllis."

"She seemed not to believe much the day I talked with her."

"It was nice of you to call on her. She enjoyed it. We both attended Saint Hilary's when we were kids."

"Yes, she told me."

"What's it like now?"

"Come and find out."

Frank O'Rourke smiled. At least that was the kind of remark you expected from a priest. Dowling was a tough bird to figure out. His matter-of-factness about the true identity of a putative yardman was deflating. O'Rourke would have thought that his discoverer would spread the news wildly, shout it to the skies, and, before or after, come breathlessly into his presence, the legendary Frank O'Rourke redivivus. Imagine what some of the people who pestered Phyl would do if they realized that the object of their consuming interest was out on the lawn clipping the hedge or in an apartment over the garage proving to himself he could no longer write in the way that had captured hearts?

The two men fell silent and in the silence heard a repetitive, slapping sound. From the window they looked out at a young man jogging up the driveway toward the pool.

"Who's that?" O'Rourke asked. "Do you know him?"

The priest seemed oddly agitated as he stepped back from the window and avoided Frank O'Rourke's eyes.

"His name is Paul Gardiner."

29

THE MOTEL in which Paul Gardiner was currently registered occupied the top two stories of the First Prairie Bank, an undistinguished high-rise building that dominated what editorial writers of the *Messenger* were wont to refer to as the Fox River skyline. In the downtown area, little separated earth from sky in the aftermath of the various projects of urban renewal that had leveled block after block, replacing taxable properties with expanses of asphalt and surrealistic multilevel garages. What was called The Mall was suggestive of a movie set for low-budget pictures, meant to be seen as blurred background or from carefully chosen camera angles. Now it was exposed to relentless daylight, a long narrow roof carried stiltlike by steel pillars between a block of shops, not quite covering the sidewalks and obscuring the identifying signs of places of business.

Horvath dropped down the ramp into the garage below

the bank building where in semishadow Officer Hanson and Peanuts awaited them.

"Have you gone up?" Keegan asked Hanson.

"I been up," Peanuts replied.

Hanson said, "After I called in, I waited right here. That elevator is an express to the floors the motel is on."

"He ain't in," Peanuts said.

"How did you find him, Pianone?"

"I been tailing him, Captain."

"I see. When did you start doing that?"

Peanuts squinted in thought. "Couple days ago. I dunno."

"Where did you first see him?"

"At Mr. Tuttle's."

Keegan looked at Horvath. "Is Tuttle his lawyer, Pianone?"

Peanuts shook his head. "He was putting the bite on one of Tuttle's clients. Then he robbed Tuttle. Tuttle told me to keep an eye on him."

"Who the hell are you working for, Peanuts, Tuttle or us?"

Peanuts did not hesitate. "Both."

Hanson said, "I don't think he realized there was an APB on Gardiner, Captain. I ran into him and we started to talk and he told me what he was doing and mentioned that Gardiner was in this motel and I checked and he's registered so I called in."

"Good work, Hanson," Keegan said. It was either this hearty remark to Hanson or strangling Pianone. "Cy, go pick up Tuttle. I want to talk to that s.o.b. And don't let him wear that damned Irish hat. It's the end of June, for crying out loud."

Keegan left Hanson in the basement garage, in case Gardiner's car was there and he came down some other way than by the elevator, or, if he was out, so he would have an appropriate reception when he returned. With Pianone, he took the elevator to the top floor and the reception desk.

"He's out," Peanuts said on the ride up.

"You already said that."

"He drove out while I was talking to Hanson. I was going to go after him but Hanson said to stay here."

"Did you tell Hanson it was Gardiner's car?"

Peanuts shook his head.

"Do you have the make and license number?"

Amazingly, Peanuts did. At the desk, the first thing Keegan did was to phone in the description of the car and the number of its license. It was an Indiana plate.

"Not that it matters," Keegan said. "Most likely it's a rental."

"Is something wrong, sir?" The clerk's tone indicated that any wrong afoot there in the lobby of the Mesa Motel could be imputed to the large, determined man who had just used his telephone without so much as a by-your-leave.

Keegan showed him his badge. "What room is Paul Gardiner in?"

"Twelve twenty-four," Peanuts said.

"Take me there," Keegan said to the clerk.

"Now, see here."

"Would you like us to break the door down?"

Keegan took Pianone's elbow and started across the lobby toward a stairway leading to the twelfth floor. The clerk, armed ostentatiously with a key, caught up with them.

"I will let you in. Under protest."

Keegan nodded. Of course, the kid was right. He didn't have to let them see Gardiner's room, and if they broke down the door he or his employers could sue them to a fare-thee-well. On the other hand, why shouldn't he cooperate with law-enforcement officers and not be so damned legalistic or whatever his attitude was?

"Perhaps the party's in," the clerk said. He might have been wishing rain on Keegan's picnic.

"Perhaps."

"He went out," Peanuts said.

The clerk knocked on the door with one hand while he inserted his master key in the lock with the other. There was no answer, even after the door was opened. Keegan had pushed the clerk to one side, got out his gun, and kicked the door open. Without warning, Peanuts barreled past him into the room. It was empty. The clerk now stood in the doorway with his mouth open. Peanuts made a quick circuit of the room and came to a stop beside Keegan. What had gotten into him? Perhaps seeing a door kicked open had awakened memories of some exercise at the police academy.

"Good work," Keegan said, for the second time in ten minutes, this time for the benefit of the clerk.

"Transfer any calls for me to this number. Captain Keegan."

"Yes sir."

"That's all."

Keegan closed the door and, having sent Peanuts out on the balcony to enjoy the view of the Fox River skyline, he began looking around. There were two double beds in the room. Gardiner was using the one nearest the door: the pillows had been taken from beneath the spread and propped against the headboard. Watching television? No, reading. A typescript lay on the bed as if put down when Gardiner left.

On the other bed lay a suitcase. Odd. Why hadn't he put it in the rack provided for it in the ensemble that included dresser and television stand and desk as well as the luggage space?

Inside the suitcase were clothes. Nothing else. The goodies were in the bottom drawer of the dresser. A canvas tote bag. Keegan put the suitcase on the floor and dumped the contents of the bag on the bed. There were two books and papers, lots of papers, typewritten. A glance at them told Keegan they were like the letter he had received from Frank O'Rourke. One of the books was an old diary and the other was some sort of record book. Keegan opened it and stared at it in disbelief.

"Saint Hilary's Parish," he read aloud. "What the hell?"

The ringing phone brought Peanuts in from the balcony and he stood at attention while Keegan answered.

"There's a call for you, Captain."

"Put it through."

The message was brief. Paul Gardiner's car had been found, parked on the river road, empty.

"I told you he left," Peanuts said.

"Yeah," Keegan replied.

When they came into the lobby, a woman with half a dozen bracelets on each arm stepped away from the desk and confronted Keegan.

"Excuse me, Flo. I'm in a hurry."

"And I represent the press." Her mascaraed lashes beat time to this announcement.

"I can't talk to you now."

Keegan tried to go around her but she stepped sideways and again looked up at him. He had the absurd feeling she was giving him dancing lessons. Peanuts came up and took the woman by the arm. God knows what he might have done if Keegan had not told him it was all right.

"You're looking for Paul Gardiner," Flo Eberle said.

"That's right. Look, come along if you want to, but I have to go."

"Have you found him?"

"His car."

"I'll come along." Keegan didn't like it, but he did not like the seeming alternatives: doing the box step with Flo there in the lobby or unleashing Peanuts on her.

"Do you know who he is?" she asked in the elevator.

"You do?"

"I do," she said smugly. "My story is on the wire, so I can tell you. He is the son of Greta Vanden!"

Keegan considered that. Peanuts' face was expressionless. "Who is Greta Vanden?"

"You cannot be serious." She drew back from him, widening her eyes as much as the heavy make-up permitted. "You are! Aren't you a fan?"

"She plays tennis," Peanuts said. "She's the one with the frills."

"She is a movie actress!" Flo's tone tolerated no more nonsense. "She is a famous movie actress and you know it. Paul Gardiner is her son."

"That doesn't help us much, Flo, but thanks."

"Doesn't it? Aren't you investigating the death of Mrs. Emil Mackin?"

"What's the connection?"

The doors of the elevator opened and they came out into the garage. Hanson stood by. Keegan traded him for Peanuts. With Cy gone, he needed a more reliable driver than Pianone. He sat next to Hanson and put Flo in the back seat.

"The connection between Paul Gardiner and Mrs. Emil Mackin, Captain, is this. Will you for heaven's sake listen!"

Keegan put an arm over the back of the seat and turned to look at her. "I'm listening."

"Paul Gardiner is the son of the late Frank O'Rourke."

"Paul *Gardiner*?"

"His son by his first wife, Lorraine. Greta is his stepmother. Her husband—her second husband—was Gardiner."

Keegan turned away and stared out the window. "Frank O'Rourke's son."

"Phyllis Mackin's nephew."

Had Phyllis even known the man was in town?

30

AFTER he parked the car, he got out and began to bounce up and down on the toes of his running shoes. He wore shorts and a sweat shirt, the sleeves of which had been cut off. A headband completed the costume. A jogger. One of thousands, hundreds of thousands, perhaps millions.

He started up River Drive, beginning in the street, then going up the curb to the sidewalk. He lifted his knees high, he kept his arms close to his sides, he ran. It was, he had found, the best disguise. Only a few years ago, the sight of a running man would have attracted notice and caused concern. Now no one so much as looked at him. He kept his eyes straight ahead. The essence of running is self-absorption. He had run all over this city, starting from different points, the motels where he had stayed selected carefully for their locations. Before coming he had pored over maps of the city, but now those printed grids had been translated into images of Fox River. He had come to know it well. He hated it.

This is where the famous stranger who had been his father grew up, this was the city that prided itself on having been his birthplace, this was where the drunken sister of the great artist lived a life of ease on the profits of her brother's work.

The house, when he had first seen it, was even worse than he had imagined. Luxurious. Practically an estate. She was the only one the famous Frank O'Rourke had provided for. Tom had been a fool to resume the family name; Paul had tried to stop him from doing it.

"Gardiner wasn't our real father."

"And Frank O'Rourke was?"

"Biologically, yes."

"At least I remember seeing Gardiner, Tom. Do you have any memories of Frank O'Rourke?"

Tom claimed he had, vague but real. Paul did not believe him. Tom wanted praise for the step he had taken, reclaiming the name he had been born with; apparently he did not realize he was trying to cash in on his father's fame. Had the man even remembered the two sons he had sired? The mention in his will was on the level of insult. "My children by Lorraine Dolan, two sons, a third of my estate to be equally divided between them." Why the hell couldn't he have said a sixth to each and mentioned them by name? But a sixth or a third of nothing is nothing. At least Tom had not lived long enough to see what their father had thought of them.

Paul, in charge of arrangements, insisted on burying his brother under a headstone that read: Thomas Gardiner.

Now, with a name other than his father's, jogging along the river road in Fox River, Paul Gardiner was, he realized, the last of the O'Rourkes, at least as far as the immediate branch went. His mother was dead, his father was dead, his brother was dead, his aunt was dead. That left Paul Gardiner, the unknown son of Frank O'Rourke.

When he had come to Fox River, he had wanted both to conceal himself and to announce to the skies who he was and why he was here. But his objective was as ambiguous as his attitude toward himself. Did he want to destroy what his father had left behind or take possession of it as rightful owner? Before he could destroy, if that is what he meant to do, he had to possess, so he had been collecting. And what a mixed bag local O'Rourkiana turned out to be.

Letters that were not genuine.

A diary of little interest.

The parish record that included Frank O'Rourke's first marriage. Paul Gardiner could not abide the thought that some day this simple ledger might be propped up and gawked at by admirers of the man who had deserted his wife and sons. How could what he had written make up for what he had been?

Paul Gardiner had read his father's work, all of it, everything he could get his hands on, read it slowly and carefully and was left utterly unmoved. Every sentence seemed a message to him from beyond the grave and, so read, the short stories and novels of Frank O'Rourke were grievously disappointing. Paul had listened to lecturers speak in awe of his father's work and it had been all he could do not to leap to his feet and remind the audience that his father had been a son of a bitch.

He tried to forget the connection.

He told himself he was Paul Gardiner, son of Sylvester Gardiner and his wife Greta Vanden, who was now married to a man half her age named Pizzaro. His new identity was scarcely a moral improvement. But people had stopped oh-ing and ah-ing over Greta Vanden. She was a pathetic forgotten woman who lived in obscurity in Burbank. Who could resent someone like that for her inability to stay married or to pay attention to kids she had inherited from a previous husband?

Frank O'Rourke in death was beyond personal criticism, it seemed. His life was described either in clinically non-judgmental terms or with a tone of grudging admiration. The artist as free spirit, unbound by the rules that govern the lives of mere mortals.

When he first jogged past the Mackin house, the lawn mower was stopped and a priest was talking to the operator. The car in the driveway must belong to the priest. Paul Gardiner jogged slowly past. He would go to the Stratton Bridge and then come back again.

Had Florey tried to deceive or was he really stupid enough to think the pages he had turned over to Feehan represented the famous unfinished novel?

Or was Feehan responsible, perhaps handing on something different from what he had received from Florey? That made more sense; Feehan, after all, was a master of the bogus. He might have decided to try his hand at imitation on O'Rourke fiction after his success with the letters. Of course, any moderately knowledgeable student of Frank O'Rourke's work would recognize these pages as an inept variation on a story entitled "On the Ocean." There existed some parodies of Frank O'Rourke's work, none really good, but infinitely better than the pages Feehan had given him. They had been contained in a Manila envelope bearing the name of the law firm of which Florey was a member.

Florey at first refused to take his call but Gardiner had persisted and finally got through.

"The pages you gave Feehan are fake."

A sigh over the wire. "They are not fake. They are quite genuine."

"They are not by Frank O'Rourke. They are not the opening of a novel."

"You're only half right. They're his, all right, but there is no unfinished novel."

"That's a lie."

"Gardiner, take my advice. Settle for what you've already managed to extort."

"I want that unfinished novel."

"Gardiner, this is my last word. I was Mrs. Mackin's lawyer. Mrs. Mackin is dead. I have lost a client. Everything she owned goes to her husband. I am not his lawyer. He is gaga. Perhaps the court will appoint me his lawyer. Perhaps not. I am not sure I would accept. I am tired of Frank O'Rourke, Gardiner, deathly sick of him. The point is this. I have no legal access to the papers. If there is an unfinished novel in that cabinet, I could not find it."

That cabinet. The phrase stuck in Gardiner's mind. He let Florey go. He let go too of his intention to get even with Feehan for being the conduit through which those useless pages had come. He would go to the source. The Mackin house and the file cabinet in the den.

He assumed Florey meant the cabinet in the den. The cabinet he had been going through last Tuesday night, Wednesday morning actually, when Paul Gardiner, in street clothes but wearing his running shoes, had stood at the window watching him.

How drunk his aunt had been to mistake him for a man Florey's age.

When he jogged back up the river road from the Stratton Bridge he did not hear the sound of the lawn mower as he approached the Mackin house. He slowed his pace. The smell of newly mown grass was sweet on the summer air. The lawn was done, the tractor gone. And the car that had been in the drive was also gone.

Paul Gardiner turned in the driveway and jogged slowly toward the house. The blue-green surface of the swimming pool glistened painfully in the afternoon sun.

31

"WHO IS Paul Gardiner?" Frank O'Rourke asked.

The question seemed to pursue Roger Dowling downstairs, and when he came across the flagstone apron of the pool and saw no sign of Gardiner he wondered if he had jogged away again. When O'Rourke had asked the question, Roger Dowling made a dismissing gesture.

"One of your fans, I think."

"Good God, you're not going to tell people who I am, are you?"

"Of course not."

And then he left, but it was not O'Rourke's concern for his own recognition that bothered Dowling as much as the fact that he did not recognize his own son. It was like a Greek tragedy of the more complicated sort, with none of the characters knowing the true identity of the others. This real-life anonymity struck Roger Dowling as infinitely sad, the son not knowing his father was still alive, the father not recognizing his son. Of course, it was romantic to imagine that after a lapse of a quarter of a century a man would recognize a half-remembered infant in a young man jogging some thirty yards away. Was it really surprising that no one had recognized Frank O'Rourke in the bearded yardman at the Mackin house? The only one who was likely to blame himself for not doing so would be Phil Keegan, and Roger Dowling could now see no reason why his friend must know.

Even before he reached the street, he had the sense of going in the wrong direction. Young Gardiner had not jogged up the driveway simply in order to jog back down again. He had turned in for a purpose. Nonetheless, testing his original hunch, Roger Dowling went out to the street and looked in both directions. Not even a sprinter could have disappeared so quickly. Roger Dowling looked back across the lawn, through the trees, at the house.

The French doors that looked out on the pool were closed, but a corner of the drape emerged from them like a pennant. It was the sort of thing Roger Dowling was certain he would have noticed when he drove past on his way down to the garage. He had looked as he passed it, marveling at how the loss of an occupant can seem to alter the appearance of a house. That corner of the drape had not been caught in the door then. Emil Mackin? According to Herman—perhaps it was better still to think of him thus, lest his secret be given away unwittingly—the invalid master was being looked after by Kevin, Kevin who referred to him as the Blob. Roger Dowling wondered where the cook had been when Emil Mackin knocked him down with his motorized wheelchair. His hand and elbow gave him pain, but not as much as his legs, where the chair had struck him just above the knees. Had Kevin taken Mr. Mackin inside and caught the drape in the door in doing so?

The French doors were not locked. He had not thought

they would be. He opened them slowly, remaining outside. The corner of the drape, released, disappeared within and the drapes, caught in the onrush of outside air, streamed across the den as if to catch Paul Gardiner in their ghostly embrace. Gardiner turned from the file cabinet, eyes wide with surprise and fear. Roger Dowling realized that the other could not recognize him against the light.

"It's Father Dowling, Paul. From Saint Hilary's. You remember."

He stepped inside and pulled the doors shut behind him.

"In search of more of your father's things?"

Paul Gardiner seemed almost relieved. "Who told you?"

"It's really not that difficult to learn. What are you looking for?"

Gardiner brought a finger to his lips. "There may be others in the house."

"There are. Why are you nervous?"

"You're a cool one. What are you doing here, anyway? But you're right about me, I came to get what I can of my father's stuff. I'd particulary like his unfinished novel."

"Why?"

"To destroy it."

"Ah. I thought it might be something like that. May I suggest an easier route?"

"To what?"

"To taking possession of everything of your father's your aunt had."

"My aunt!"

"She was, you know. That's my point. You must have heard of her husband's condition. He's not compos mentis, scarcely in a position to inherit anything. That leaves you, doesn't it? Are there any other O'Rourkes?"

Paul Gardiner listened and then, smiling slightly, pulled out the desk chair and sat. "I never thought of that."

"What you need is a lawyer. I would be very surprised if you were not awarded custody of Emil Mackin, this house and its contents, everything."

"I don't want the house."

"Just your father's writings?"

Paul Gardiner swung toward the desk. He seemed to find it distasteful to have his obsession mentioned.

"You will never succeed in erasing him from American literature, Paul. Not even God can alter the past. Besides, why ask everyone else to forget him when you can't yourself?"

"Forget him? I don't even remember him. He's a name, that's all, a reputation, a figure in literature courses."

"You didn't know your Aunt Phyllis either, did you?"

"Don't call her that."

"She was killed, Paul. Murdered."

"I read the papers."

"Is that how you learned of her death?"

"Oh, come on." Gardiner laughed, but he looked up at Roger Dowling with something of the fear he had shown when the priest first entered the den.

"You realize the police are looking for you, don't you? Now. They've learned what motel you're staying in."

"Big deal. I'm not hiding."

"Why did you move?"

"What do you mean?"

"I know you stayed in the Motel motel. For one night. Why did you leave?"

"Did you see the place?"

"I was there, yes."

"Then why ask why I moved?"

"You did register under your own name."

"Yes. Paul Gardiner." He said it with emphasis, lest there be any doubt in Dowling's mind what his name was. "Are you serious about the police?"

Roger Dowling nodded. "Think of it, Paul. You come to town, you go everywhere making a point of your interest in Frank O'Rourke. Except when you came to Saint Hilary's, of course. Why didn't you tell me what you were really looking for?"

"To avoid your saying what you said anyway. Wanting to know how I was raised. Wouldn't you have thought the son of Frank O'Rourke should be a Catholic?"

Roger Dowling smiled. "I think everyone should be a Catholic."

"Well, I'm not and I didn't want to go into it."

"What did you do with the parish records?"

"I've got them, don't worry."

"In your motel?"

Paul Gardiner nodded. He might have been realizing then that, if the police had gone to his motel, if they searched his room, everything he had stolen would be found.

"Where is your car, Paul? You have a car, don't you?"

They heard the siren, then, far off, but neither of them seemed to doubt that it was coming toward the Mackin house. Roger Dowling certainly did not doubt it. Paul Gardiner was on his feet, looking around a bit wildly.

"Do they know I'm here? Did you tell them?"

"Where is your car parked?"

Didn't he realize this was the explanation of his being located? The sound of the siren rose as if shortly it would ascend to levels perceptible only by animals other than men. The piercing sound seemed aimed at them, at this house. Paul Gardiner's expression became wilder and he pushed past Father Dowling and was standing in the open French doors when the police car came up the driveway with its siren become a guttural growl and its rooflight revolving, sending red blips of light like a coded accompaniment to the dying siren.

Paul Gardiner bolted. He took off around the pool, running not like a jogger but like a man escaping the scene of the crime. The uniformed officer who had jumped from the car shouted after him: "Halt! Halt where you are!" He had undone the flap of his holster and now, incredibly, there was a gun in his hand.

Roger Dowling saw the gun even as he saw Phil Keegan emerge from the other door. There was a woman too, behind the armed officer. She was fairly jumping up and down with excitement as she pointed after the fleeing figure. Father Dowling recognized Flo Eberle.

"That's him," she cried. "That's him."

It was the sight of the gun that propelled Father Dowling, a gun that seemed the focal element in the tableau that formed so quickly around the halted police car. The priest started after Paul Gardiner, to stop him, to shield him, to prevent his doing anything that would justify the use of the gun.

With the agility of a regular runner, if not the grace, Paul Gardiner was already around the pool and on his way across the great expanse of the lawn, heading in the direction of the river. To run was like an admission of guilt and, pursuing Gardiner, Father Dowling could hear behind him the shouts of Keegan and the officer. Flo Eberle's shrill voice was also audible. The voices blended to give the impression of baying dogs.

Suddenly the figure of Herman was visible ahead. He must have rounded the garage and come onto the lawn from the far end. Where he now stood was on the line Paul Gardiner was taking toward the river. It was an absurd destination. Gardiner would come to a sheer drop and have to turn and face his pursuers. Though that was all to the good, so long as he did nothing to provoke the firing of a gun.

Herman retreated before Paul Gardiner, backing toward the bluff, his arms out before him in an odd fashion. As Paul Gardiner came closer, Herman crouched, and the pose he was taking was unmistakable. Football practice. The open field tackle. Herman maneuvered to get more surely into Paul Gardiner's line.

"I'll get him," he shouted, and his voice might have been drifting across a playing field from decades before. "I'll get him. He's mine."

The triumphant voice and that absurdly crouching would-be tackler seemed to enrage Paul Gardiner. There was little doubt he was headed right toward Herman.

"Stop," Father Dowling called. "Paul, for God's sake, stop!"

But nothing could stop them now, the angry trapped man, the older man with half-remembered delusions of gridiron grandeur. When Paul approached, Herman came out of the crouch and stood upright and he was in that position when Paul Gardiner bowled into him, stiff-arming the older man as if he were participating in his fantasy. Contact stopped Paul Gardiner. Herman staggered backward. On the edge of the bluff, he paused, his arms flailing wildly, and then he was gone from sight, replaced by a dwindling cry of terror as he went down.

Paul Gardiner stepped back from the cliff and turned as Father Dowling came up. The priest ignored him. He went over the side, starting down after Herman, slipping and sliding, long grass bending beneath him, creating a slippery slide down which he scudded on his heels, hands and arms bumping along on the almost sheer face of the cliff. He could see Herman below, his body bent over the cyclone fence. He had struck it with his back and still faced upward, as if he were watching the priest come slipping and sliding down to him. Roger Dowling put out his hands and came to a jarring stop at the fence.

O'Rourke's back looked broken. Roger Dowling looked into his eyes. They seemed unseeing, but he found a pulse.

"Are you sorry for your sins?" he whispered in Frank O'Rourke's ear.

There was no response.

"I am going to give you absolution for your sins."

A sound emerged from the writer's mouth, and blood bubbled forth, making it difficult to interpret it as speech. Roger Dowling lifted his hand and traced a blessing over Frank O'Rourke. *"Ego te absolvo ab omnibus censuris et peccatis in nomine patris, et filii, et spiritus sancti, amen."*

When he sought a pulse now he could not find it.

Shouts above, the sound of a gun—it was like listening in on earth from some more favored vantage point and for a fleeting moment Roger Dowling envied Frank O'Rourke for his escape from it. He considered easing the body off the fence, but decided he should not. Phil Keegan's voice emerged from the cacophony above.

"Roger, are you all right?"

He did not answer at first, letting Phil repeat the question. The interval was a private wake for Frank O'Rourke. "God rest your soul," Roger Dowling whispered into the unhearing ear. "May you be granted eternal peace."

"I'm all right," he called.

"How's Hermie?"

Hermie. Roger Dowling lifted his voice again. "He's dead, Phil."

He waited there until they came down for him, descending like monkeys or mountain climbers, helping him into the harness and hauling him up. Paul Gardiner was there, handcuffed to an officer, when they brought the body up.

Roger Dowling could not resist looking at Paul's face

when the young man saw the body come over the brow of the cliff. It seemed a moment when some terrible Epiphany must take place, the abandoned son recognizing the long-lost father, and the true understanding of what had just occurred dawning on him.

But this did not happen. Paul Gardiner turned away, as if in distaste, as if the bearded man had betrayed some peculiar flaw by being mortal.

"Well, son," Keegan said, "that makes two."

"Two what?" Gardiner growled.

"Bodies. First Mrs. Mackin, now this poor old guy. Get him out of here, Hanson."

A protest died on Gardiner's lips and he was led away to a police car. Keegan turned to Roger Dowling and put his hand on his shoulder.

"You don't look so good yourself."

The priest looked at his clothes. He was a mess. One trouser leg had caught on a branch and tore as he went down the cliff and the calf of his leg was bleeding. His hands still smarted from the spill he had taken by the pool when Emil Mackin ran into him. Roger Dowling felt a sudden vertigo as the events of the past hour rushed through his mind. He put out his hand to steady himself, intending to lean on a tree. Phil Keegan caught him or he would have fallen, and, supported by his old friend, the priest was helped across the lawn to the ambulance. Keegan insisted he had to be checked over.

"You might have broken something, Roger. You might have been killed."

It occurred to him that, if he had, there would have been no priest to shrive him. He could do for others what he could not do for himself. A priest too needs a priest. He seemed to have babbled this aloud.

"So do doctors," the man leaning over him said. "Need doctors, I mean."

Later Roger Dowling would realize he had been in shock.

" 'Human kind cannot bear very much reality.' " This quotation, too, he spoke aloud.

The hovering face grew fuzzy, receded, was gone.

32

"Why did he run if he's innocent?" Phil Keegan demanded.

"No one is innocent. He had lied and stolen and misrepresented himself, he had reason to run. But not the reason you want. He didn't kill Mrs. Mackin."

"How do you know that, by private revelation?"

Roger Dowling smiled. "Phil, you have to prove him guilty. I can assume he's innocent."

"We both saw him bowl Hermie over that cliff."

"The man was trying to tackle him. They collided. The older man was thrown back. The fact that there was a cliff . . ."

"All right, all right. Is it okay if I have another beer?"

While Phil was in the kitchen, Roger Dowling filled a pipe and touched a match to it. It was several days after the incident at the Mackin house, and the fact that Herman had not yet been identified as Frank O'Rourke suggested he would not be. Father Dowling prayed that young Paul Gardiner need never know that, accident or not, he had been the cause of his father's death. His hand went out to touch the breviary lying on the table beside his chair. Second vespers. Frank O'Rourke had had two evenings to his life, one anticipated, one real. But Father Dowling thought of a phrase from Compline, *custodi nos dormientes*, guard us while we sleep; it seemed an epitaph for Frank O'Rourke. And he thought again of the son.

Gardiner's attitude toward his father might permit him to be unaffected by this knowledge, but the priest doubted it. The son had been too intensely interested in every aspect of his father's career for hatred to be a sufficient explanation of the quest that had brought him fatefully to Fox River, Illinois. The anger and resentment were directed at the deprivations of his youth; what he had wanted was his father's love. To discover it had been Frank O'Rourke who had made that pathetic effort to tackle him and had paid for it with his life would be too heavy a burden for the son to bear. Roger Dowling saw no moral obligation to reveal to Paul Gardiner or anyone else the true identity of the Mackin yardman.

"We've already charged Gardiner with murder," Keegan said when he returned with a bottle of beer. He sat in the easy chair across from Roger Dowling and poured beer slowly into a glass tipped at a 45° angle.

"What evidence do you have?"

"He admits having been there at the time, but only because he claims to have seen Bill Florey at the house."

"Does he also admit having made anonymous calls to the police telling you that?"

Keegan shook his head. "As a matter of fact, he denies it."

"Your caller did say Florey was at the Mackin house that Tuesday night, didn't he?"

"We already knew that."

"That Florey was there earlier and left at nine. But that isn't why the man telephoned you. I wonder who he was. Chances are he was at the house too."

"That would make three."

"So you think Florey went back?"

"His wife as much as told Horvath, but her testimony can not be used. Florey, Gardiner, and the mysterious caller."

"But why would Florey kill his client? That makes no sense, Phil."

Keegan looked at the priest in exasperation. "You're holding out for the unknown caller, is that it? Roger, you always find excuses for a suspect we know. It's Florey or Gardiner."

"Or Kevin. Or even Herman. Why not? That was a strange household, Phil. Who knows what resentments might have festered there."

Roger Dowling did not fear that Kevin would be jeopardized by such speculation. Nor did he fear for Paul Gardiner or William Florey. His own experience at the hospital, together with the reading of Phelps's report on Mrs. Mackin, had told Roger Dowling the likely killer of Frank O'Rourke's sister.

Phyllis Mackin had had severe bruises on her upper legs, just above the knee, exactly like those Roger Dowling had received when Emil Mackin ran into him with his motorized wheelchair. Phelps assured Keegan that her bruises had been sustained at the time of death and were as recent as the blow to her head that had rendered her unconscious. Roger Dowling, by taking Kevin's charge that Florey had been having an affair with Mrs. Mackin and adding the presence of the lawyer at the house later that night, could imagine a scene by the pool that would enrage the woman's husband, if he saw it, if he were capable of understanding it. No one suspected Emil Mackin, though he was always present at the scene. Why should anyone suspect a man so obviously out of touch with reality and scarcely in control of himself? Yet Roger Dowling thought otherwise. Mackin's helplessness was almost a caricature and it did not square with his obvious ability to get around in his wheelchair. Not that Roger was surprised Phil Keegan's attention had not been turned to Emil Mackin, either in the matter of the mysterious phone call or of far more serious things.

The previous day, Roger Dowling had visited the Mackin house. Kevin was staying on.

"Someone has to take care of the Blob."

"Who pays you?"

"Florey. I won't pretend I'm not curious about Phyllis's will. She just had to leave me something."

"Paul Gardiner will be the principal heir."

Kevin snickered. "A lot of good it will do him."

Emil Mackin sat in his chair by the pool, seemingly staring into its blue-green depths. When Roger Dowling approached, the head began to bob and weave.

"I'm going in for cigarettes," Kevin said. "Would you keep an eye on the Blob?"

Roger Dowling stood behind the chair, gripping the handles. He spoke over the gyrating head with its wild tufts of hair.

"I will speak out only if an innocent person seems in danger of paying for what you have done, Mr. Mackin. Meanwhile, you might think about the only judge who matters."

There was no indication that these words were understood, but Roger Dowling was certain they had been. No doctor he had consulted would believe that a person with Mackin's symptoms could maneuver the wheelchair in the way the priest described. How long had Mackin viewed the world from the disguise of an idiot? Hadn't his wife consulted doctors? If she had not . . . But he did not want to assign blame.

"My main fear, Roger," Phil Keegan said, "is that the prosecutor will blow it in court and no one will pay for killing Phyllis O'Rourke."

"A perfect crime?"

"There are no perfect crimes. Only dumb prosecutors or impressionable juries."

Roger Dowling did not question his old friend's anger. But Phil knew as well as he did that in many cases there was not even the arrest of a suspect. Still, he was right to say there are no perfect crimes, not if perfect means undetected. What had Phyllis Mackin called it? An eye in the sky. There were worse metaphors for the one who watches over us all, seeing the best and worst, seeing everything.

"Roger, that unfinished novel we heard about. It was found in Hermie's apartment over the garage. He must have been reading it."

"Hmmm."

"A funny thing, he was trying to write himself. Imagine. The yardman. Florey says it was pretty bad stuff."

"He would know."

"He also says that the unfinished novel, when it's published will make a bundle."

"Will it be published?"

Keegan put down his glass and wiped foam from his lips. "Florey says it should have been published long ago. An unfinished novel! It's a shame Frank never finished it."

"I'm sure he felt the same way," Roger Dowling said.